KiNG OF THE DANCEHALL

KiNG OF THE DANCEHALL

NICK CANNON

ST. MARTIN'S GRIFFIN
NEW YORK

Published in the United States by St. Martin's Griffin, an imprint of St. Martin's Publishing Group

KING OF THE DANCEHALL. Copyright © 2018 by Nick Cannon. All rights reserved. Printed in the United States of America. For information, address St. Martin's Publishing Group, 120 Broadway, New York, NY 10271.

www.stmartins.com

Designed by Devan Norman

The Library of Congress has cataloged the first St. Martin's Griffin edition as follows:

Names: Cannon, Nick, 1980– author.
Title: King of the dancehall / Nick Cannon.
Other titles: King of the dancehall (Motion picture)
Description: First edition. | New York : St. Martin's Griffin, 2018. | Tie-in for the film, The king of the dancehall.
Identifiers: LCCN 2018001447 | ISBN 978-1-250-11324-5 (trade pbk.) | ISBN 978-1-250-11325-2 (ebook)
Classification: LCC PS3603.A553 K55 2018 | DDC 813/.6—dc23
LC record available at https://lccn.loc.gov/2018001447

ISBN 978-1-250-82456-1 (trade paperback)

Our books may be purchased in bulk for promotional, educational, or business use. Please contact your local bookseller or the Macmillan Corporate and Premium Sales Department at 1-800-221-7945, extension 5442, or by email at MacmillanSpecialMarkets@macmillan.com.

Second St. Martin's Griffin Edition: 2023

10   9   8   7   6   5   4   3   2   1

KiNG OF THE DANCEHALL

FREEDOM

I still remember the very moment that I tasted freedom again. Five years locked away up north in the bowels of New York's prison system, so far from home, had made me numb. I was desensitized. My days were spent working out in the yard doing a hundred push-ups at a time, reading ghetto love stories, and trying not to think about what I was missing. But, the morning I heard the guard call out my name—"Tarzan Brixton, it's time!"—I started to feel alive again. As I walked down my cell block for the last time, my heart beat faster than usual. The sun seemed to shine brighter than it ever had before. I had to squint my eyes as I stepped outside the gates for the last time. I felt momentarily blinded by the light. By the joy I felt at being free for the first time in so many years.

I had suffered through a five-year bid, locked down in the belly of the beast over some light work. Armed robbery charges and resisting arrest. I ran up in a store on Linden Boulevard and stuck up the clerk at gunpoint. Of course there was a fucking off-duty cop in the store buying lotto tickets. He tried to be a hero, pulled out his badge, yelled out "Freeze!" and all that dramatic shit. I shot out of there like a bullet, flying down the block like Usain Bolt. The part that hurt the most was that I almost got away. But, I was running too fast, and I tripped over my own feet when I tried to turn a corner at the last second. It gave the cop enough time to catch up to me, and before I knew it I was on my way to jail. It pissed me off because it was my own fault. Not just because I was the one who had committed the crime. But because it was my own clumsiness that got me caught. I was usually so light on my feet, a skill I used to my benefit in my life of crime. I had been in countless chases like that one before, and each time I had gotten away. But life has a way of catching up with you.

It wasn't even a major jux. Just a quick way to get my hands on some cash because my mama was in a desperate situation. Sounds typical, I know. But, there's nothing typical about me. My mother made sure of that when she named me Tarzan, after the legendary king of the jungle. Ironic that I found myself caged in a place with some of the most vicious animals imaginable. I survived because I was strong, raised by one of the toughest women on God's green earth. My mama, Loretta Brixton. It was to her home that I returned immediately after being released from prison. I needed to see her, to hug her, see her smile again. But, I wasn't prepared for the sight that greeted me when I stepped across the threshold of our apartment in the Brooklyn projects that we had called home my whole life.

The place wasn't as spotless as it normally was. The living room looked a little messy, and there were dishes piled up in the sink. Leftover food sat on top of the stove, and as I looked around I could sense that Mama wasn't her usual self. My mother had been sick for a long time. It was one of the reasons I had robbed that store. She had suffered from diabetes since I was a kid. It was something she had always struggled with. But, then her kidneys had failed one after the other in the years before I went away. The doctors placed her on dialysis several times a week, and put her on medication. But with each hospitalization, the bills piled higher and things got thick. I needed the money I was going after in that robbery to set things right again. For a little while, at least.

I'm not trying to say that I was a saint. Far from it. My motives weren't all pure. I wanted to flex a little. Grab enough cash to get Mama straight and get a few nice things for myself. Stunt in the hood for a change. Times had been hard for a long time. I felt that I was overdue for my turn in the spotlight. Still, selfish motives aside, my main focus was on getting the money Mama needed for all the hospital stays, holistic treatments, and medication it took to treat her kidney failure and diabetes.

Growing up in the tough streets of Brooklyn with no pops was tough. Mama had her hands full with me. I had always been a live wire and a magnet for trouble. That's probably the reason why Mama chain-smokes Newports like there's no tomorrow. She ain't afraid of a little dark liquor, either. Growing up, all of my boys were afraid of my mother. But, I never was. Mama was sweet. Underneath that tough, unsmiling exterior was a heart of pure gold.

I walked into her bedroom and found her lying in bed. She seemed to be asleep, but I couldn't be sure. Her breathing was steady, and the room was dead silent. It felt kinda spooky. I looked at all the pill bottles scattered on the nightstand. Gauze, bandages, and needles for her insulin injections. Her Bible was there, too. Just like it always was. That made me smile.

I cleared my throat, announcing my presence. "Hello, Mama. Your prodigal son has returned."

She opened her eyes and saw me there. Slowly, she sat up in the bed, and leaned forward. Her eyes welled up with tears.

"Aww, Mama, don't cry."

She shook her head at me, the tears streaming down her face now. She snatched a tissue from the box at her bedside. "Little boy, if you don't get over here!"

I rushed over and hugged her tighter than I ever had before. I felt like a kid happy to see their mama after a tough day at school. I had been to the school all right. The school of hard knocks. And it had been one hell of a lesson to learn.

Mama reached over to her nightstand and grabbed a cigarette.

I protested. "I thought the doctor told you to quit smoking."

"Child, hush!" She lit it and took a long pull. "Cigarettes keep my stress level down. Unlike you."

That hurt.

She wasn't done. "Five years away and now you want to come back into my house and tell me what to do?" She sucked her teeth hard, her Jamaican way. She had been born on that picturesque tropical island in the West Indies. But she immigrated to Brooklyn in her youth. She had always been a trailblazer that way. Brave. All of her family was back home. But she had come to America hoping to get her shot at the dream. Sadly, it wasn't going well.

"Ma, I made some mistakes. I admit it. But, you know I love you."

She grunted.

I sat there in silence watching her smoke. The guilt that had gnawed at me like a ravenous dog for the past five years was back again. I had let my family down.

I never set out to be the bad guy. Nobody grows up aspiring to be a troublemaker. The problem was that I couldn't do the things that usually get dudes like me out of the hood. I couldn't rap. Couldn't play basketball. But, what I could do was get money by any means. The hustle came naturally to me. It was as much a part of my DNA as the blood that ran through my veins.

"You love me. Okay. But, were you thinking about me when you were doing all that mess out there in the streets? Lawyer fees, bail money, all of that on top of the bills that already litter the area! Did you care about my health then, boy?"

"Yeah." It was the truth. I had never stopped caring. True, I had let her down. I had spent the past five years dealing with that. But, I was just a boy trying to learn how to be a man. It was obvious that Mama didn't understand that at all.

I heard someone walk in behind me, and I turned to see my little brother Trent standing there. He looked like my twin. Our resemblance was unmistakable. He wore a McDonald's uniform, a baseball cap, and a scowl.

He looked me up and down. "They finally let you out, huh?"

I stared at him for a minute. "That's how you greet your brother? You ain't happy to see me?"

"Thrilled." His expression told me the opposite.

Trent was nineteen years old, with the maturity of a man twice his age. Our four-year age difference made it hard enough to connect with each other. But being in two very different places for the past five years had made things even more awkward between us. Trent was smart. Not just smart, but *really* brilliant. He could have gone to Harvard or Yale if he'd had the opportunity. But, that wasn't possible. Not with our mother sick, me locked up, and money scarce. He had enrolled in a local college, but dropped out in order to work full-time and help make ends meet. I could hardly look at him without feeling guilty. I knew that my time away had made it even harder on him.

"Why you ain't never write me?" I knew the answer when I asked it. But, I had to say something to fill the awkward silence.

"Write you to say what? How I'm out here working double shifts at McDonald's when I should be in college? How you've got our mother literally worried sick over your dumb ass?"

His words stung, but I didn't react.

"Trenton!" Mama checked him.

Trent looked at her and apologized under his breath. He looked at me, and held up a crumpled bag of food. "You hungry? Want a burger?"

I walked over to him, snatched the bag out of his hand, and gave him a big hug. His protests were muffled by my armpits as I pulled him even closer.

"Get off me!"

"I missed you, little bro!"

He pretended like he didn't want my affection. But, I could tell he had missed me, too.

"Let me go, Tarzan! I ain't with all that homo shit." He finally wiggled free. He wiped his face where I planted a big wet kiss. He shook his head in disgust. "They really put it on you in there, huh?"

I laughed, and grabbed him again.

"Ma, get him off me. He's changed. I think he's trying to grab my booty! Your son's a batty boy!"

I laughed even louder. I knew he was playing. There was nothing sweet about me. "You know what they say in prison. 'Don't ask, don't tell.'" I winked at him.

Trent shook his head at me and walked toward the door. "First of all, genius, that was a military phrase, not a prison reference." He shook his head. "You really are the world's dumbest criminal."

"I'll still kick your little smart ass, though."

"Try it." He kept walking toward the door.

My reaction was instant. I threw the bag full of cheeseburgers at him, and hit him hard in the back of the head.

Trent spun around, his arms raised defensively. "Mama!"

I was laughing while my mother sat shaking her head at both of us.

"You two are foolish. Ya act like children. What am I going to do with both of you living under the same roof again?" She rolled her eyes, and let out a sigh. She couldn't hide her smile, though.

Trent left to change out of his work clothes.

Mama looked at me. "I can't have all of this commotion in my house. I ain't in the business of taking care of grown men. I can barely take care of myself."

"Don't worry, Ma. I'm going to figure it out. I'm going to take care of all of us."

She gave me that look that I hate. The one where she seems to see right through me. "Like you did when you went running in that place waving a pistol around like some wannabe badman?"

"Trust me," I said. "I'm done with that life. I'll be honest with you. I'm not sure what I'm going to do. But, I definitely know it won't be *that* again. I promise. I'm going to be different. Better. The new and improved Tarzan Brixton."

She shook her head again, finished off her cigarette, and closed her eyes. She looked so tired. She seemed to be mumbling something, and I leaned closer to hear her. I realized that she was praying.

"Lord . . . Heavenly Father, help him. Gracious God, guide him down the righteous path. Use my son for your works."

Throughout my life, I could always remember my mother praying. It was her form of warfare against the threats that came against her family. Against the diabetes that forced her to maintain a strict diet. Against the kidney disease that had ravaged her body. And now it seemed that she was calling on God to fix me. To help me get my shit together once and for all. I had my doubts about religion. It didn't seem real to me. For all her praying, fasting, and Bible reading, it seemed that our family couldn't catch a break. I was beginning to wonder if God was listening to Mama at all.

Her voice drifted off, and once again she lay there silently with her eyes closed. This time I could tell that she was sleeping. I could hear her snoring softly. I kissed her on the forehead, turned off the light, and left the room.

I went looking for Trent, and found him lying across his twin-sized bed, also sleeping. I watched him for a minute, amazed at how grown he was now. When I got locked up, Trent had just been entering high school. His voice had just started changing, and he had been a little boy who idolized his big brother. All of that had changed now. Trent looked like a carbon copy of me, except his life was uncluttered by all of the bullshit that I couldn't ever seem to shake loose. Seeing the growth in my kid brother was a reminder of the amount of time that had passed since I went away. I turned out the light and shut his door behind me as I left.

I hit the streets. I had some unfinished business out there. Despite my charming personality, I had always rolled solo for the most part. Getting caught up with crews and gangs was a sure way to get caught up in bullshit. So, I was an army of one out there in those Brooklyn streets. My dude Kareem was my only real friend. We had grown up together, and like me, Kareem liked to get money with as little pomp and circumstance as possible. For that reason, he and I worked well together. We often let each other know about the get-money schemes we got exposed to. And it was for that very purpose that I sought him out that day.

As I walked through the Pink Houses, a housing project in East New York, Brooklyn, I was shocked by how different everything looked. The complex's cute name masked a very ugly reality. I had seen some terrible things in these projects. It had made me a man and, sadly, gave me all the preparation I needed for jail.

As I walked to my girl Tameka's building, I looked around at how things had changed. The fashion was definitely different. Guys were wearing their jeans a lot tighter and black women were rocking their natural hair. What really amazed me was the fact that so many of the white girls had butts. The presence of white people on the perimeter of the projects was a new sight, too. It was like they weren't afraid of us anymore. It had me bugging as I walked down the block.

I found my boys exactly where I had left them five years ago. They had changed clothes. A couple of them looked like they had aged a bit. But, for the most part, they all looked like somebody had pressed the Pause button on the day that I got locked up, and not much had changed with these guys.

I greeted them and smiled with pride as they gave me hood hugs and welcomed me home. It felt good to be back among my friends. Although the letters and commissary had been nonexistent coming from them, I didn't hold a grudge. Everybody had his own life to live, and there were no hard feelings.

I hit the blunt they were passing, and Kareem got my attention.

"We got some work for you if you're trying to get back on." He eyed me closely.

I appreciated that. I nodded.

He shrugged. "You just came off a long bid, so I understand if you want to lay low for a while."

I was already high, but I took another puff. "I told myself I was gonna come home and do the right thing. But, my moms is sick. My brother needs some help holding it down for her financially. So, yeah. I need to get back in the mix as soon as possible." I passed the blunt to the next man in the cipher.

Kareem nodded. He was my friend, so I knew he understood where I was coming from. Like me, Kareem grew up in a household with no father figure. It forced us both to be the man of the house whether we were ready or not.

"What you about to do now?" he asked.

"I'm on my way up to Tameka's house to see my daughter."

I saw the expressions on all of their faces change. They exchanged glances, but nobody said anything.

"What's the problem?"

They all shrugged their shoulders, and shook their heads. Kareem passed me the blunt again.

"When's the last time you heard from her?"

I inhaled. "Right before I got locked up."

The fellas laughed. I knew it sounded crazy.

"That's why I'm on my way up there now. I need some answers. And I want to see my daughter."

I saw Kareem glance at me strangely, but we all got distracted by a girl walking by with an unbelievable ass. Until she rounded the corner out of sight, every one of us was dumbstruck.

I passed the blunt back to Kareem. "Yo, I'm out. I'll come back and talk to you later after I check on my daughter."

I headed up the block toward Tameka's building, floating from the effects of the first weed I had smoked in five years.

TAMEKA

Tameka was a girl I knew from around the way. Not just any girl. Tameka had a body that would make a good man do bad things. I've always had a weakness for women like that. The kind who turn heads and break hearts all without batting a pretty little eyelash.

I got with Tameka right before I got locked up. Every guy in the hood had wanted her. She was fresh meat back then. Young, vibrant, and ready to go. We had all grown up with her, and in a lot of ways she was like our little sis. But, then she blossomed and her body went from zero to one hundred. Her titties popped out all perky and succulent. Her waist and hips took on a sexy curve that made other girls jealous. And then there was that ass. That ASS!

And she only had eyes for me. It was a no-brainer. I locked that down. I was proud to call her my girl and flaunt her around the hood. That body stopped traffic, and she had the attitude to match. A couple of months went by and before I knew it, she was pregnant. My daughter Tisa was born, and my whole life changed. It made me really want to man up and be a good provider. I guess that was another reason why I was out there putting in work. Hustling for my family. My moms, my baby, and my baby moms.

Tameka was supposed to be my ride-or-die, down-for-whatever girl. But, the whole time I was away, I hadn't heard a word from her. My mother had reached out to her. But, Tameka hardly ever brought Tisa over to visit her even though the women lived feet apart. It was like she had forgot all about me the minute the judge banged his gavel at my sentencing hearing.

I climbed the stairs to her second-floor apartment and pounded on the door. I could hear movement inside, but no one answered. I knocked again, even louder this time.

"Tameka! Come on. Quit playing and open this goddamn door!"

"No!"

I heard her high-pitched voice.

"Yo, Tameka, let me see my daughter. I ain't playing with you! Five years, and no letters, no visits. And now you can't even have the decency to let me see my baby?"

I banged on the door again. Finally, she opened it just a crack. The guard chain kept it secured.

She looked prettier and thicker than ever. I had to try hard not to smile.

"Fool, 'the baby' is six now." She looked at me like I stunk. It was obvious that she was not happy to see me. I began to realize, with great disappointment, that I was probably not getting any pussy today.

"So what? She's still *my* baby."

Tameka gave me a strange look. "No, Tarzan. She is not."

I stared at her. I could feel my pulse racing. I took a deep breath. I hoped that she was playing.

"What the fuck did you just say?"

"You heard me!" The bitch was unapologetic. "She is not your daughter. That's why I didn't visit or write. Because there was no point." She chewed her gum hard. "Found out a few months before you got locked up that Tisa belonged to Charles and not you."

I felt a surge of rage rushing through my body. Thoughts of that little girl, and of Tameka, too, had gotten me through the past few years. Now here she was telling me that it was all a lie. I tasted blood.

"Bitch!" My voice echoed off the walls in the project hallway. My mama would have slapped the shit out of me if she heard me call a woman that. But, this time it was accurate. "I should snap your fucking scrawny ass neck! Charles? Really? That fucking scrub!"

"Whatever! You know what, Tarzan? Yes. Charles is my man now. And, lucky me. Because he's someone that can actually take care of us. Unlike your trifling incarcerated ass!"

"That nigga was doing the same shit I was doing!" My voice echoed again. One of her nosy neighbors peeked out their door. "Mind your business!" I yelled. They slammed the door shut.

"Not no more, Tarzan." Tameka's voice was mocking now. "Charles is a boss. I don't have to worry about nothing. Bills paid, Tisa in private school, car, clothes, groceries. And, I get my hair did every week!"

"Tameka, you're bald-headed!" I was looking right at her.

"So what?" She stared at me with hatred in her eyes. "You make me fucking sick! Why don't you just get away from my door? Yelling and making all this damn noise! You gonna wake Charles up."

My eyes flew wide. "The nigga's here?"

I didn't even give her a chance to answer. Once again, I saw red. I reacted instantly, and kicked the door with all my might. The chain gave way easily, and I rushed past Tameka into the apartment. I saw the scared expression on her face and wondered what happened to all the mouth she had a minute ago. But, she wasn't my target. I wanted to get my hands on Charles. The dude used to be a friend of mine. And now he had taken my girl *and* my daughter. I was furious.

I rushed through her living room and saw the leather couches, the flat-screen TV on the wall. It was obvious that Charles had been hooking her up. I saw a triple beam scale on the kitchen table, surrounded by some cocaine and a bunch of cash. I shook my head, grateful now that I didn't have a child growing up in the midst of this mess. But, I was still gonna kick Charles's ass.

Tameka was still behind me, screaming and yelling for Charles to help her. I rushed toward the bedroom and kicked in the door. Charles was lying in the bed sleeping in nothing but his boxer shorts. I punched him in the face and he woke up, dazed and confused. I hit him again, twice, and he struggled to gain his composure. Disoriented, he tried to reach for his Glock 9mm on the nightstand. But, I got to it first. I used it to beat the shit out of him. I beat him for stealing the woman and child I had convinced myself were mine. I beat him for the years I spent separated from my family. I beat him until he was unconscious, sprawled out in a puddle of his own blood on the floor.

I looked around for Tameka and found her standing in the kitchen crying with a butcher knife in her hand.

"Please don't hurt me." Tears streamed down her face. She looked petrified.

In that moment, I felt like I was at a fork in the road. One part of me wanted to slap the shit out of this broad and send her flying into the wall. The other part of me wanted to grab her by the face and stick my tongue down her throat. After all, it had been five years since I felt the warmth of a woman's body. But Tameka wasn't worth any kind of emotion. Not my passion or my rage. As heartbroken as I was, I couldn't let her have the satisfaction of seeing that shit. Believing that Tisa was my daughter had gotten me through some of the toughest moments of my incarceration. In my mind, that little girl was the only good thing I had ever done in this world. Discovering that it was all a lie had crushed me. But, I wasn't going to hurt this bitch. Moms had taught me better than that. Instead, I walked over to the table and snatched up all the money I could grab. I filled up each one of my pockets with cash and walked right past Tameka, out the door.

I got to the lobby, exited the building, and calmly walked through the courtyard. I could hear Tameka yelling at me from her window. She wasn't scared anymore now that I was leaving.

"You ain't shit, Tarzan! You are a bitch! Nothing but a worthless, punk ass piece of shit!"

She was tossing shit out the window at me. I could hear glass shattering behind me, but I just kept walking.

"You're gonna get yours, Tarzan! Wait until Charles wakes up. This whole city is gonna be looking for your bitch ass! You're a dead man! Watch!"

I quickened my pace and started a slow jog. She was making it hot. A dollar van slowed down near me, and I jumped inside. I had a pocket full of cash and no plan. I had to think fast.

ON THE RUN

My first day back on the streets, and I already got myself into more trouble than I could handle. I knew how fast word traveled in the hood and that my name was being mentioned all over Brooklyn. Charles was a bitch. I wasn't too worried about him. But, I had been gone for a long time. The hierarchy of the streets was constantly changing. Because of the money he was making, and who he was making it for, Charles had connections that I didn't have the luxury of. So, it was necessary for me to get low and stay that way for the time being. I got to Linden Boulevard and found a pay phone. I was surprised to find one, and even more shocked that it was working. With a phone card I bought from a bodega, I frantically dialed my cousin Toasta's international number.

My cousin answered the phone, and it sounded like complete pandemonium on his end of the line. I could hear kids playing in the background, a baby screaming, a woman yelling. Over the noise, Toasta's gravelly voice barked into the phone.

"Who dis? Ouch! What di hell?" It sounded like he got hit with something, and he cried out in protest. "Peta Gaye! Can't you see me on the phone here?" He yelled at his wife some more, and then returned to the phone. "Me say who dis?"

"Toasta! It's your cousin, Tarzan."

"Tarzan? Brethren! Wha g'wan?"

"Yo, what the hell is all that noise in the background?" I was struggling to hear him over all the commotion.

"Ugh! Ya know who it is. Baby mama on that bullshit again."

I laughed at the irony. "Brother, you're preaching to the deacon!"

Toasta laughed, his voice booming in my ear. "Man, I miss Brooklyn! What I wouldn't give to be on the block right now with a slice in one hand and a fatty in the other!"

"Don't let Peta Gaye hear you say that shit. I already hear her giving you hell in the background."

He laughed again. "So, they finally let the lion out of the cage, huh, brother? What's the plan now?"

"Yo, fam, I gotta get the fuck out of Brooklyn ASAP! Like tonight. Word. I need to lay low for a while."

"Uh-huh. What happened?"

I wasn't about to get into all that over the phone. "Long story, my dude. But, I just came up on about five grand that we can flip. If I can get down there, you can link me up with a plug, and we put that shit back out on the streets up here. Double, triple up real quick." I had actually snatched about seventy-five hundred from Charles's bitch ass. But, I figured it would take a good two grand to get everything lined up quickly. I needed to leave Mama with some money, get some clothes and ID, and get a plane ticket.

"Say no more, cousin. You need to lay low? I'm the king of laying low. You can stay with me. Everything is lovely here. You know I got the whole island on lock."

"Yo, good looking out, Toasta. Word! I'm on the next thing smoking. I'll hit you back when I get to the airport. Make sure you answer your phone."

"No doubt."

"Peace."

I got a seedy motel room on the cusp of the city and got low for the rest of the day. I got my hands on a trap phone and got word to Kareem that I was all right. He let me know that Charles had put the word out that I was a dead man. My mama's apartment was allegedly being watched, and there was no way I could go back there. Not that I was scared to face Charles. He was a sucka nigga who I had no problem going to war with. But, the last thing Mama needed was bloodshed at her doorstep. Instead of going home, I called home and talked to Trent.

"Bro, I need you to get some paperwork together and come meet me. And don't tell Mama."

I could hear the frown on his face over the phone. "What kind of paperwork?" He sucked his teeth. "You're in trouble already, aren't you?"

I was offended even though it was true. "I need your help, Trent. You got my back or not?"

There was silence on the other end of the phone. I prayed that he would hold me down.

Finally, he asked, "What do you need?"

I laid it out for him. An hour later, he met me at the Atlantic Avenue subway station. I had never been more relieved to see my brother walking toward me. I spotted him maneuvering through the crowd, his face set in a grimace. He didn't look happy to see me, but I didn't care. I had bigger problems than that at the moment.

"Thanks for coming. You brought my papers?"

He nodded, and shoved a manila envelope in my direction. "Here."

I snatched it up, and rifled through it to make sure everything was there. He had done exactly what I asked. I smiled at him. "Thank you, Trent. You don't know how you're saving my life right now!"

He nodded. "Kareem said niggas are looking for you. What did you do now? You just got home!"

I shook my head. "Some bullshit with Tameka. I had to put my hands on that clown Charles. Apparently, Tisa's not even my daughter." I didn't look at him when I said it because I was embarrassed to admit that. Tameka had played me.

Trent laughed a little. He shook his head. "Mama told you she was trifling. You should have never got caught up with her."

"I know that now," I said. "But, with Charles looking for me I gotta get out of town for a little while."

Trent frowned. "Charles is a punk. You had a fight, and he lost. What's the big deal?"

There was no way I could tell Trent that I had robbed this nigga for his stash. No way. "It's complicated."

I handed him a white envelope. "Give this to Mommy. Tell her I love her, and I'll be back soon."

Trent stared at me, clutching the envelope in his hand. In his eyes I saw a whole bunch of questions, maybe even a few accusations. But, to my relief, he tucked the envelope in his jacket pocket, nodded, and didn't question me further. He did leave me with some youthful words of wisdom.

"I know I didn't show it. But I was glad to have you home. It would have been nice to try to connect again after all this time. But, I'm also glad to see you go."

I didn't like how that sounded.

"If you're in danger, I want you to go somewhere so you can be safe."

I nodded.

"We grew up hard," he said. "You made some mistakes. But, you have a family that loves you. Don't forget that." He extended his hand to me, and I took it. "Take care of yourself."

I pulled him into a hug, and this time he didn't protest. I wondered how long it would be before I would see my little brother again, and tried not to get choked up.

"You, too," I managed. "Take care of Mama."

He left, and I watched him go. I felt so proud of him, and so guilty for not being a good son like he was. One who stayed out of trouble and followed the rules. But I was a badman. There seemed to be no redemption for me.

I rummaged through the papers Trent had brought for me. Inside the envelope, Trent had tucked his U.S. passport. I prayed that our resemblance was strong enough for me to pull this off. With Trent's passport in hand, I went to the DMV nearby and got my hands on a New York State ID in his name. Kareem had tucked an online boarding pass for a flight to Kingston, Jamaica, into the envelope with all the papers Trent had brought me. I hated that Kareem told my brother about the trouble I was in. But, I understood why he did it. Charles had a point to prove in the hood now. It was important that my brother be on point to protect himself and Mama in case that fool came gunning.

I was weighed down with guilt. Every time I thought about the situation I had placed my family in, I was sick with myself. It felt like I always wound up here. Paying for some stupid, spontaneous decision I had made in a split second. My hood survivor instincts would kick in, and I would lose my temper. That was when things usually went too far. This time, though, I was in too deep. I was fresh out of jail, supposed to be laying low. Instead, I was running around Brooklyn like a fugitive with a price on my head.

I thought about the money I had stolen and what the consequences might be if Charles and his niggas got their hands on me. All my life I had operated with a fearlessness that frustrated and perplexed my mother. I never worried about the very real possibility of my demise. Whether I was running up in a store with a loaded gun, entering a house to burglarize it, or pistol whipping a drug dealer who disrespected me, I was never scared. But, as my mother often reminded me, I didn't have to be scared to get hurt.

"There's a whole lot of people who weren't scared laying in the cemetery right now," she often said.

I thought about that now as I faced my reflection in the mirror in my motel room. I knew that I wasn't immortal. But, I never believed that I could be touched. I was Tarzan motherfucking Brixton. Even with the weight of the world on my shoulders, I knew that I would figure a way out of this. Somehow, I would make it work.

I got my next couple of moves mapped out, grabbed something to eat, and went back to the motel and crashed. I was exhausted. The front desk gave me a wake-up call at

5:00 A.M., and I grabbed my ticket, the cash, and the few possessions I had to my name. I headed for the airport and hopped on the next flight headed for Kingston. I was putting all my faith in Toasta and I prayed that he wouldn't let me down.

CLEAN SLATE

I landed in Kingston, navigated that long-ass line through customs, and waited in the sweltering heat for my cousin to come and get me. I hadn't been to Jamaica in a very long time. Not since Trenton and I were kids and my mom had brought us to visit her homeland. It felt different now that I was a grown man, on my own. Beautiful green hills kissed the skyline. I looked around and took in all the scenery while I waited outside of the airport for Toasta. I was anxious to see him again.

Toasta had become a part of our family for a few years when we were kids. My aunt Cheryl had sent him to stay with us in Brooklyn when he was ten years old. She wanted him to get a better education than the one he was getting in Kingston. That was when Toasta and I had gotten close. His real name was Allester, but we all called him Toasta. He liked to front like he got the nickname "from carrying the biggest hot-fire gun in Brooklyn." But, that's not how I remember it. I recall our family calling him that as a kid because he would always walk around the projects chewing on a piece of day-old bread. He added the "All Star" when he moved back down to Jamaica and started deejaying. For years, the locals called the emcees "toasters." So it all made sense.

I stood in the heat, watching the locals and the arriving visitors for about an hour. The energy of this place felt very different from what I was used to back in Brooklyn. There was a spirit here that seemed to fill every inch of the island, from the weather to the people that inhabited it. A spirit of heat, sex, and danger, all wrapped up in one enticing package. I could sense the excitement that awaited me here, and I anxiously glanced around for signs of my cousin. Then finally, an old, rusty eighties edition of a BMW 325i pulled up. The hood of the car was painted a completely different color from the rest of it. It sputtered and coughed as it came to a halt, and I stood in shock as my cousin climbed his big ass out of it.

"Sim-simma! Who got the keys to my Beamer?" His smile rivaled the sunshine.

"I don't think that car is what Beenie Man was talking about when he wrote that line."

Toasta laughed and gave me a strong hug.

"Wha' g'wan, General?" Toasta looked larger than life. Six-two full of energy. His eyes sparkled as he looked at me after so many years.

"Man, it's good to see you, cousin."

"Yeah! Yo, how's Aunt Loretta?" he asked.

I thought again of my mother who I had left behind in New York. "Could be better. You know what I'm saying? But, we're about to help her with that, right?"

"No doubt." He rubbed his hands together, dramatically. "We'll have this ting oiled up in no time. I already started having the conversations. We can probably even move a little work around here in Kingston, too." Toasta seemed excited by the prospect. "You can make a decent business of it, ya knawmean?" He gestured toward his raggedy ride. "Let's get out of this heat. We 'bout to take over, little bro!"

I laughed as we walked toward the car. "I thought you said you already took over a long time ago. What happened to all the stories you told me when I was locked up? When I got down here we were gonna be riding around in brand-new cars, flashy jewelry, champagne. Big chains, dollars, and Ducatis. Where is all of that, Toast?"

He put my bags in the trunk. "Patience, brethren. Patience!"

We climbed inside the car. He looked at me, smiling.

"I like to blend in with di common folk. Appear to be frugal for my people. Jesus was meek, ya know?"

I bust out laughing. "Jesus wouldn't even put his bumper sticker on this piece of shit!"

"Watch your mouth!" He sucked his teeth extra hard, and then we both cracked up laughing at the same time. Meanwhile, his Beamer put-putted down the Kingston highway. The voice of the deejay boomed from the car radio.

"Wha' g'wan, Kingston? We have Raddy Rich in the studio! He's the man everyone is predicting to be the winner of the In the Dance Clash Battle. This is Jamaica's big televised dancehall competition for ten million dollars! *Big money*, man! Say hello to the people, Raddy Rich."

"Wha' g'wan, Jamaica?"

I couldn't believe my ears. "Ten million dollars? That shit can't be right."

Toasta laughed. "Ten million *Jamaican* dollars. That's a bit less than a hundred grand in the U.S."

I nodded. Still, that was one hell of a grand prize.

Toasta interrupted the broadcast, popping in one of his own mixtapes instead. He turned up the radio and blasted the music through the car's cheap speakers. He shouted over the music with a huge grin on his face.

"I made this tape last week. Pure fire!" He danced in his seat while driving, which cracked me up.

"I might not be the baller I described in all my letters," Toasta said. "But, I got this dancehall scene sewn up. Ya g'wan see. I told you when I came back down here that I wasn't playing no games. I meant what I said. I'm serious about this music ting, ya heard?"

I heard him loud and clear. Once Toasta graduated from high school, he left my mama's house in Brooklyn and came back to Jamaica. He had made up his mind that he was going to be the next Shabba Ranks. He came home and started rocking parties. That was almost ten years ago, and he's been grinding in these Kingston streets ever since. It appeared that nothing major had popped off yet. A wife and a house full of kids later, he made a living selling mixtapes and spinning records at the local dancehalls to make ends meet.

I nodded. "I hear you, cousin."

Toasta pulled up at the curb and parked the car. I frowned, still recognizing this house even though I hadn't been here in many years.

"What are we doing at Aunt Cheryl's house?"

Toasta shook his head. "This is where we're staying. Peta Gaye kicked me out last night."

I stepped back in shock. Toasta and Peta Gaye had been together for years. "Why? What happened?"

He shrugged and shifted his weight from one leg to the other. "She said she don't have room for you, me, her, her sister, and all our kids." He sucked his teeth. "So, we're staying here."

I felt bad. "What? Seriously?"

He nodded.

I shook my head. "Yo . . . I'm sorry, Toast." Then I remembered all the things he was saying in those letters he had written me while I was locked up. "Yeah. We taking over. Balling out of control! Living with your mama. Big up!"

Toasta rolled his eyes and walked toward the house while I laughed behind his back.

"Big tings!"

Aunt Cheryl's house was a small one in the Jamaican province of Hellshire. What it lacked in size, it delivered in charm. We were greeted by Aunt Cheryl the moment we crossed the threshold.

I smiled wide at the sight of her. Aunt Cheryl was straight from *yard* with the thickest Jamaican accent I ever heard. Just like Mama, she seldom smiled, but had a heart of gold. Aunt Cheryl would give her family and friends the shirt off her back. She was my mother's younger sister by four years. Family legend was that Aunt Cheryl hadn't smiled since Christmas of 1979. That was the year when her husband hit the local lottery. Uncle Remis had been his wife's punching bag for years, enduring her verbal and physical attacks for the duration of their marriage. He had often encouraged his wife to lighten up, have fun, and smile. She never managed to do any of that until the money came. Uncle Remis later ran off with a young Chinese lady who smiled all the time.

Aunt Cheryl hugged me and grumbled under her breath in Jamaican patois. I understood enough to gather that she wanted me to follow her. So, I left my bags by the front door and followed her into the kitchen. The small space was filled with a smell so divine that my stomach started growling instantly. She was preparing a large pot of rice and peas.

"Coo yah," she said.

I smiled. My mama used the same term all the time. It meant, *"Look here!"*

"Rice and peas. Ya wan' eat? Empty bag can't stan' up! Nuff tings for man to nah know 'bout life and be mawga skinny, ya know. Rice and peas. Di bikkle is pon de table! Eat!"

I tried to keep up with what she was saying, but my mind was reeling.

She placed two big steaming bowls of rice and peas on the table in front of us. I didn't hesitate to dig into the *bikkle*, which meant food. Aunt Cheryl made the best rice and peas of all. Typically, it was reserved for Sunday dinners. But, Aunt Cheryl would make some at the drop of a hat. No cookbook or recipe needed. Perfection every time, with just the right amount of coconut and thyme.

"Thank you, Mother. Bless."

"Thank you, Aunt Cheryl."

"Tarzan," she said. She stood staring down at me, both hands on her wide hips. "Ya stay 'ere, ya fetch up a job. Mi do mi sista dis favor. But ya nah freeload pon mi like an idle jubie. Ya understand?"

I nodded. "Yes, ma'am."

I understood perfectly. In my mother's and Aunt Cheryl's eyes, there was nothing worse than an *idle jubie*. A lazy kid.

"I'm here to work hard, Aunt Cheryl. I'll be on my best behavior."

"Mi nah bawn back a cow!"

That meant she's not stupid. So don't try to play her. But, I wasn't. I started to protest, but she walked back to the stove, mumbling and cursing to herself.

"She's so happy to see you," Toasta said.

"I can tell."

He laughed. "Yo, finish up. Drop your things off in the back room. We got a few runs to make before we hit the dancehall tonight."

"We sleeping on your old bunk beds?" I was joking.

"Damn right," he said. "Thought you'd be used to that style. Wanted to make you feel at home like in your old prison cell."

"Oh, word? Now you want to crack prison jokes? Okay."

"And I got the top bunk, so don't even start that shit. You not going to be pissing on me in the middle of the night like back in the day."

"No matter where I sleep, I'm still going to *piss* on you!"

"Cho! No one g'wan piss pon no one in dis house!" Aunt Cheryl shouted from the stove.

"Yes, Aunt Cheryl!" I called back.

Toasta pointed and laughed in silence at me being scolded like a kid. I flipped him the bird with both hands.

We finished eating and I was shocked to find out that Toasta wasn't playing. The old bunk beds were still in his old bedroom, just like back in the days when we were kids. The difference was that now Toasta was nearly three hundred pounds. It was hard to imagine sleeping in such close quarters and in such intense heat with his big ass.

Still, I was grateful for a place to stay. I remembered the trouble that had sent me fleeing from Brooklyn in the first place. If this was where I had to stay for the time being, I would make the most of it. I put my shit down, and me and Toasta headed out into the streets of Kingston.

WORK WILL WORK

We walked a short distance down a few long dirt roads lined on either side with colorful brick walls. This wasn't Trench Town. But, we were definitely in the hood. Several shanty homes dotted the road, and the sound of children playing and laughing filled the air. It got louder as we neared his house at the end of a dirt road.

"Daddy!"

The children charged at Toast full speed. I smiled and stepped back as they rushed him, giggling and jumping all over him. Toasta was laughing, too. Finally, he got them all to calm down enough for us to proceed toward the house.

Peta Gaye sat on the porch of the zinc house. Reggae music played from a small boom box placed on top of a brick wall. Peta Gaye's skin glistened with sweat as she fanned herself in the shade. She smiled as she watched her two older children do a fresh choreographed routine they had come up with. The younger children joined in and all the adults hyped them up, encouraging them. Everyone gathered around was impressed by the talent these young children possessed.

"Big up! Ya see dat nah? Mi kids di best dancers in di J-A! They mash up di place!"

Toasta's kids beamed with pride hearing their daddy's praise.

"Daddy, we missed you. Where have you been?" "Don't make Mommy mad anymore."

Toasta squirmed, hearing his children's words. "I'm just a couple of houses down at Grandma's house."

His daughter frowned. "Grandma mean. We nah like over there."

I nodded in agreement.

Toasta changed the subject.

"Peta Gaye, wha' g'wan? How's mi empress?"

She didn't answer. She just rolled her eyes and continued nursing her newborn with a shawl covering her torso for modesty.

A woman emerged from the house, and I swear it felt like time stood still. I had never laid eyes on a more regal woman in my lifetime. She looked younger than Peta Gaye, but had the same smooth, chocolate brown skin. She wore her dreadlocks tied up in a colorful head wrap. It had the appearance of a beautiful crown towering on top of her head. She wore a long dress that fully covered her body, and a long rosary around her neck. Her body was toned and thick, her natural beauty shining through even in such conservative clothing.

We locked eyes. She didn't look away. I *couldn't* look away.

Toasta broke the silence. "Tarzan, this is Maya, Peta Gaye's younger sister."

I snapped out of my trance and cleared my throat. I extended my hand to her.

"Nice to meet you," she said, sweetly. Her voice sounded like music. She looked at me, staring at my Timbs and my Yankees fitted baseball cap. I realized I wasn't dressed like the other men on the island. I hoped that was a good thing.

"The pleasure is all mine." I was smiling so hard that she looked away, embarrassed.

"Easy, boy! She's the bishop's daughter." Toasta's eyes were wide as he warned me.

"The bishop?" I looked at her.

"Mi father runs the church here in town."

I nodded. "Respect."

"Ya name Tarzan ya say?"

I nodded again. She giggled.

"What's so funny? You laughing at my name?"

"Nah, man. It's just mi never met anyone named Tarzan before."

"Well, I've never met anyone so beautiful before."

She smiled, shyly.

Toasta laughed louder than he had to. "This guy needs some practice with women." He interrupted our conversation with his jokes. He turned to his oldest son. "Son, don't ever use any tired game like you just heard. Ya hear me?"

The boy nodded.

"You'll be single for the rest of your life if you listen to Tarzan."

I knew my cousin was making fun of me. But, at that moment I didn't even hear what he was saying. My soul was awakened! I was in the presence of an angel, and I knew it. I was meeting her for the first time, but already it was clear that Maya was nothing like my ex Tameka. In fact, she was the exact opposite of my usual type. And I loved it. I hadn't known her for more than thirty seconds and she already had me. Until then, I thought that "love at first sight" was bullshit. But there was no other way to describe this feeling.

Toasta kissed Peta Gaye on the forehead. She just rolled her eyes and pretended not to notice.

"Let's go, Lover Man. We have an appointment we can't miss." Toasta tugged me toward the road.

I was still awestruck with Maya. She waved at me with her dainty fingers.

"Hopefully, we'll see each other around." Her voice was so melodious.

"I'll make sure of that," I said. It took a great deal of effort for me to walk away.

I followed Toasta back to his car.

"You taking me to the connect?" I asked. "This guy lives down here in Hellshire? That's what's up! 'Cause this five grand is starting to burn a hole in my pocket."

"Patience, young general! We'll work on getting you to the connect later on. First, you got to get a legitimate job."

I looked at him, confused. "What are you talking about?"

"Uncle Screechie's!"

I sucked my teeth. "You must be playing. I ain't never had a real job."

Toasta laughed. "Well, today is a new day, brethren. If you want to keep the Jamaican police off of you then you need to appear like you're being an upstanding citizen of the island. Ya know? Blend in with the people. Plus you heard what mi mother say. No idle jubie!"

We pulled up at Uncle Screechie's—an outdoor seafood restaurant right on the Jamaican shore. It wasn't much. But what it lacked in luxury, it made up for in its culture. A mixture of sand and old colorful bricks lined the perimeter. The bricks were worn, which only added to the charm of the place. Uncle Screechie had a medley of Bob Marley's music playing. The tide came in as me and Toast approached. I inhaled deeply. The scent of the ocean and the food filled my nostrils. I could hear reggae music playing softly from somewhere in the back. I looked around and smiled. I was relaxed and happy to be there. It felt like I truly belonged in Jamaica. It felt like home for the first time.

"Uncle Screechie!" Toasta called out. "We have a visitor!"

Uncle Screechie emerged from the back of the restaurant wearing a wifebeater, a pair of khaki shorts, and sandals. He was in his fifties, tall and slender with a thick patois.

"General! Tap a di tap! Wha' g'wan? Peace and blessings!"

I smiled, and gave him a strong hug and handshake. I'd loved this man since I was a young boy. He was so smooth, and had effortless swagger. I loved to hear him speak, even though it was tough to understand him sometimes. His eyes told a story of his journey through life as a rude boy who got out of the game and went legit. Retired, on the beach, running his own restaurant in a very calm and easy existence. He was living the dream.

"Uncle Screechie! How you been?" I was smiling so hard that my cheeks hurt.

Uncle Screechie filled me in on everything going on at the restaurant, while Toasta helped himself to a plate from the kitchen. I was trying to focus on what Uncle Screechie was saying, even though I could barely understand him.

"One, one coco full basket, ya know? Time longer than rope. Ya up in the States and wanna be a likkle badman. Ya nah wan' romp wit dat life. Ya nah rude boy. You a good heart."

I nodded.

"Mi hear you need a job. Allester tell me ya g'wan keep out of trouble."

"Yes, sir. You got some work for me?" I rubbed my hands together. This was exactly what I needed. Something to keep the local authorities from suspecting anything while I got my hustle cracking in these streets.

"Listen 'ere, General. Di aim of di wise is to work for pleasure, and work through di pain. *Work will work.* Neva forget dat. Ya understand, General?"

I nodded again.

"Work will work." I repeated it back to him.

Uncle Screechie smiled. "Work is growth. You get out wha' you put in, nephew. You grow when you focus on being di best human being. Every mikkle makes a mukkle."

I didn't know what the hell that meant, but I agreed with him anyway.

My uncle seemed pleased with me. He was glad that I seemed so enthusiastic about the idea of working.

He shoved a broom into my hand. "Start with the sweeping up the sand off di bank."

I was caught off guard. I stared at it like it was a foreign object I had never held before. "Right now?"

My uncle chuckled. He walked off toward the kitchen, and called out to me over his shoulder. "Work will work. It will keep ya mind off of di fuckery, General."

I looked over and saw Toasta laughing hysterically while eating his lobster tail and festival corn bread fritters that smelled delicious.

"Work will work! Hurry. Get to sweeping, man! We still got business to handle. Tonight you g'wan see your big cousin put in di real work. Bless up!"

THE DANCEHALL

Toasta schooled me on the history of dancehall on our way to the club that night.

"Dancehall is not just a style of music, Tarzan. Dancehall is a culture. It is a spirit. It has a rhythm, a soul."

I nodded. "Okay."

"First king of the dancehall was Bogle. Then come John Hype. Ding Dong. Then di dancehall went mainstream."

"You could teach a class on this shit." I laughed at Toasta. He got a twinkle in his eyes whenever he talked about it.

"It is a part of history!" he yelled. "Dancehall is an art form. It is love and war. Pleasure and pain. There's a danger to it. An intensity. *Passion*."

I laughed again. "Okay. If you say so. Sounds like all the clubs in Brooklyn that I go to all the time."

"It's nothing like that." He shook his head, seeming frustrated by my ignorance. "In the clubs in the States, the men stand around and let di women do all di work. The dancehall is a different story. Everybody gets in on the fun. It's a conversation set to music." He steered the car with ease while I watched the road. It still tripped me out that people drove on the right side here.

"Dancehall originated in the late seventies here in Kingston," he continued. "But, actual dancehalls go all the way back to the forties. They were like makeshift nightclubs for the inner city people of Kingston that couldn't participate in the uptown parties. A dancehall could literally pop up in the middle of your street. See, dancehall is the music of the people, the struggle, the grind."

"Damn. You make this shit sound wild!"

Toasta sucked his teeth. "You gotta experience it for yourself," he said.

We arrived at last in Port Royal, the beautiful harbor known around the world for its significance in high-grossing Disney movies and in history. Toasta beamed with pride.

"Port Royal was the home of the legendary pirates. So that means it was the site of many legendary parties." Toasta gestured toward the landscape as we coasted slowly through town. I looked around at all of the low-hanging palm trees, their branches gracefully brushing the earth beneath them. The port was nestled at the mouth of the Kingston Harbour, and was once the largest city in the Caribbean.

"Imagine this place crawling with pirates, women, wine, and treasures. All of dat might sound like folklore. But, it was di real ting. They used to refer to it as the 'Sodom of the New World.' Even the parrots and monkeys dat the pirates carried with dem would be drunk." He laughed. "But, di port got ravaged by an earthquake, then a tsunami, and several hurricanes destroyed di place. Many say it was the wrath of God for so many years of fuckery!"

I imagined all of that as we drove through the town. I could almost picture the scene full of half-dressed women slithering around the port, doing naughty things with the cutthroat pirates. Back in the seventeenth century this place was popping. Women, drugs, alcohol, libations, and potions. As we approached the dancehall, it was clear that not much had changed.

"'Dese days we no longer have di pirates. But, there's still plenty of badman dem. Still di same spirit. Ya' have to see for ya'self."

We parked the car and walked up to the entrance of the dancehall where we went through an intense physical search before we got in. Security practically strip searched one dude in particular. He took off his shoes, lifted his shirt, and they checked his mouth with a flashlight. Then, two security guards checked the dude's dreadlocks and found a knife.

I stood back, shocked, as the guards put the kid in a headlock and roughly tossed him off the property.

"Uh-oh," Toasta said. "Got him."

I looked around and saw several armed guards posted up on the roof wearing sunglasses and stoic expressions and toting machine guns. I felt a little apprehensive as we entered the dancehall known as The Jungle. To me, it looked like it was part brothel, part bar. The place felt eerie, erotic, dark, and mysterious. Much like the old pirate days that Toasta had described, the club had a sexual energy that was undeniable. Women stood against the wall wearing nearly nothing, their faces twisted into expressions of pure lust. Tongues flickered, ass cheeks bounced, sweat dripped. The air smelled sweet. Like pussy and baby powder. I walked through, mesmerized by what I was seeing. The place was a feast for the eyes. An actual treasure chest sat in one of the corners, full of props made to look like jewels spilling to the floor. The music was pumping, pulsating through the speakers. Dancers were gyrating across every inch of the room. I stood with my eyes wide, taking it all in.

A tall, dark-skinned man danced in the center of the floor wearing Versace sunglasses and draped in gaudy gold jewelry.

"That's Raddy Rich," Toasta said, gesturing in the dude's direction. "He's a rock star in the dancehall scene."

Raddy Rich had women all around him. He seemed unfazed by all the attention.

I nodded. "That's the dude who was talking on the radio earlier."

Toasta nodded, recalling our conversation in the car.

I could hardly believe what I was witnessing. Everyone in the dancehall was rocking, singing the lyrics, and moving on the dance floor. Outrageous hairdos, colorful bold fashion, and bodies grinding on one another. It felt like a great big orgy set to music. There was a lustful and erotic energy in the place that was impossible to ignore. I kept looking around for some niggas with patches over their eyes like the pirates my cousin had described from back in the day. It felt like I had stepped back in time to see that the real pirates of the Caribbean were definitely not rated PG.

Toasta caught me staring at a couple practically screwing against the wall. I had the sense that I should look away and give them some privacy. But, I was amazed by what I was witnessing.

"They're daggering," Toasta explained, yelling over the music. "It's a dance where the women wrap their legs around the men, while suspended in midair."

To me, it looked like dry fucking. The women humped

the floor, their bodies bouncing to the beat. Headstands, back bends, splits. Ass everywhere! I could hardly allow myself to blink out of fear that I might miss something even more outrageous. Toasta called out the names of all the dance moves. Shampoo. Bogle. Sesame Street. Whine and Dip. Bubble. Every dance was more sexual than the last. It was like twerking and gymnastics combined, and I was loving it.

"This is The Jungle, baby!" Toasta was hype.

So was I. The beat was almost deafening. Loud, distorted bass in my ears. It felt like I was in some type of dream. There were bodies everywhere. All shapes and sizes. Big girls took over the dance floor with no shame, bouncing, sweaty, sexy bodies moving to the rhythm. I was mesmerized. My gaze fell on a gorgeous, green-eyed, light-skinned beauty wearing a hot pink spandex cat suit in the center of the dance floor. She danced in perfect synchronicity with her crew of all female dancers, all dressed in neon cat suits of assorted colors and big gold earrings that glowed in the darkness.

The sexy one in the pink winded low as the crowd worshiped her. I understood it. All that ass needed to come with a seat belt! Her face was equally lovely. The people cheered and yelled, throwing their hands in the air, snapping their fingers into the shape of a gun.

"That's Lady Kaydeen," Toasta said. "She's got the best female dance crew on the island."

The crowd kept sending shots up, and the excitement was high as Kaydeen and her crew finished their performance in the center of the dance floor.

An all-male dance crew took over next. For the first time,

I realized that the dance "floor" was actually the street in the converted parking lot we were in. But, the rugged atmosphere only added to the allure of the place. I looked up and spotted armed men holding machine guns in the rafters above.

Toasta noticed me looking. "Security," he said.

I returned my attention to the dance floor and saw a crew full of Asian women. They moved like sisters! This entire scene was blowing my mind. I was sweating, and I hadn't even danced yet.

Toasta must have sensed that I needed some refreshment. He gestured for me to follow him, and we headed for the bar.

We waded through the crowd and found a spot at the bar on the far side of the club. The bartender looked like he might be a member of security, too. He wore a designer suit, his dreadlocks neatly cinched in the back, and a gun on his waist. He appeared to be a ladies' man, judging from the way he chatted up a group of ladies at one end of the bar.

"That's Casanova. He own di place."

I watched the man, intrigued. Toasta nodded his approval.

"Casanova is one of the shrewdest Jamaicans in Kingston. He penny pinches like crazy around this place. I should know because I work here all di time. But, he makes money and keeps a safe atmosphere for the people who come here to party. It gets a little crazy out here sometimes. So, Mr. Casanova runs the dancehall with brute force. Behind all the music and the dancing and drinking, it's like Rikers in here."

I looked up at the armed soldiers in the rafters again.

Casanova had a lot of finesse, but seemed to run his establishment with street tactics. Toasta summoned him over, and we watched while he reluctantly pulled himself away from the women he had been talking to. He approached with a big smile on his face, puffing on a spliff.

"Why you not up in the deejay booth?" he asked Toasta. "What, I owe you money?"

Toasta laughed. "For once, you do not owe me a dime. I'm on my way up there now. Me just wan' introduce you to mi cousin Tarzan."

I shook Casanova's hand while Toasta explained that I had just come to stay with him from Brooklyn. He asked Casanova to keep an eye out for me, and to watch my back while he went to work.

I was slightly offended. "I don't need nobody to back me up. I'm from Brooklyn. I know how to handle myself."

Toasta and Casanova laughed a little.

"See?" Toasta said. "He's a wild one. Keep an eye on him." He gave Casanova a pound and walked off toward the deejay booth.

I sucked my teeth, and ordered a Hennessy straight. I stood by the bar watching the festivities.

Toasta was now commanding the party. His energy was through the roof as he chanted into the microphone and hyped the crowd. He was up there grooving his ass off and it made me smile.

"Ja! Ja! Bruk it dung! Big up yourselves!"

The energy from the crowd was unlike anything I had witnessed before. It felt surreal—sexy, dangerous, and electrifying. The excitement was contagious.

A crew of dancers dressed alike in all white were on the

dance floor. Their T-shirts said DADA POSSE. The crowd was going crazy. Just when the roar of the crowd seemed at its height, it swelled even louder. I saw a girl with an hourglass body in a pair of skimpy Daisy Duke shorts. "Batty riders" was what the dudes standing near me were calling them. She dropped down in the middle of the floor and did a full split, bouncing at the end to the rhythm of the beat.

I tried to get a better view by standing up closer to the edge of the crowd. Now I could see that the girl getting all of the attention was Maya—the bishop's daughter!

My mouth hung open in shock. Maya's dreadlocks were swinging with the tempo of the crowd. Her dance crew joined her and they killed a choreographed routine together.

I was mesmerized by the way she moved her body. It was like her hips had a mind of their own. It was hypnotic. I couldn't believe this was Peta Gaye's little sister who I had just met earlier.

Our eyes locked, and she danced over to me with her hand extended. My heart sank. I shook my head.

"Nah. I'm good. I don't dance."

She frowned. "Oh. What you too gangsta?"

"Nah. It's not really my thing, you know?"

"Okay. You must nah be bad enough."

Now I was the one frowning. "Bad enough?"

"Only badmans rule the dance floor. Real qwenga."

"I don't even know what a 'qwenga' is."

"Hot steppa. Gangsta. Rude boy." She nodded toward some dudes standing nearby. "You see dem mans dere?"

The crew of tough-looking guys took the dance floor and started a routine.

"They run their yard. See, in Kingston, rude boys know how to move."

"Well, in Brooklyn it's not like that. Real niggas don't dance."

"Oh, I see. Mi think you might be scared, no?"

I didn't like the sound of that. "I ain't scared of nothing. Especially something this silly."

She laughed. "Silly, huh?" She turned around and pressed her ass against my body. She began to wind her hips and grind all over me.

I didn't know how to handle all that. What she was doing was typically reserved for the privacy of a bedroom.

"Come on, badman! Move dem hips."

I nervously tried to gain control of the situation. But, there was no use. Maya was working me over.

"What's wrong? I thought you weren't afraid of nothing."

"Afraid definitely isn't the emotion I'm feeling right now." I was rock hard, and the fact that I hadn't had any pussy in five years didn't help the situation. I wanted Maya in the worst way.

She turned it up another level and bent over even further and winded her hips against me. I wasn't ready. I held on to her waist for dear life. I bit my bottom lip in ecstasy and closed my eyes, gone. Thankfully, before I could embarrass myself and bust all over Maya right there on the dance floor, my cousin came over and snapped me out of it.

"Come on, boy! Ya nah ready for all o' dat!" Toasta laughed, and looked at Maya, apologetically. "I hate to interrupt your little tutorial. But, me and my cousin here have business to tend to."

I was relieved, but embarrassed at the same time. I hadn't expected to feel the way Maya had me feeling on that dance floor.

She looked up into my eyes, smiling. "It's okay. Maybe later I can show you some more. Since you're not afraid."

I stuttered, trying to come up with a good response. Toasta pulled me away, and I was aware that I had blown it.

"Man, let's go," Toasta said. "You need to thank me for coming to your rescue. She had you out there looking like a mule in heat, man!"

"Whatever! I was handling that thang. That's light work for me."

He looked down at the bulge in my pants and laughed. "Light work, ya say? Okay. That's what I always suspected."

Now I couldn't hide my embarrassment, and Toasta laughed loudly.

"I told you, brethren. Ain't nothin' like the dancehall!"

DON DADA

Toasta brought me upstairs to the upper level of the club. This was what they considered to be the VIP section. A bunch of tough-looking men with no smiles on their faces lined the edge of the balcony. They all wore black DADA POSSE jackets, creating a barricade around one particular table. The men openly carried semiautomatic handguns, staring back at me coldly as I made eye contact with them. It was clear they weren't fucking around. But, being from Brooklyn, I wasn't scared of shit. At least I told myself that I wasn't. I walked in extra hard, and returned the same venom with my own stare.

We approached the table they were blocking, and I could see the man the goons were protecting. He was a white man with a bald head and a menacing glare. He was covered in tattoos and gold jewelry. He looked like he was from the streets. But, I was thrown by the fact that he was white. I had encountered white people in Jamaica before. But, all of them were proper and polished. This one was gutter. It was written all over him.

"Who's the thugged-out white boy?" I asked.

Toasta answered in a hushed voice. "That's Donovan 'Dada' Davidson. He's the plug."

I chuckled a little. "*He's* the plug? Seriously?"

Toasta wasn't laughing. "Dada is one of Kingston's biggest dons. Everyone wants to be down with the Dada Posse. He's a gangsta by choice. And that's the worst kind, because he'll do whatever it takes to prove how ruthless he is. In reality, he grew up with an overly privileged life. His father is the European billionaire Pierce Davidson."

"Who's that?" I wasn't impressed yet.

"One of the most powerful and richest men in all of Jamaica. The Davidson family goes all the way back to the precolonization days. Old money. Super paper! Pierce Davidson owns five radio stations, three hotels, and several restaurants and gas stations. A real backra, if you let his employees tell it."

I shook my head. My mother used the term *backra* often to describe the white folks she worked for over the years. It meant a slave master; someone who worked you till your "back raw."

"Legend has it that old Pierce Davidson got his money and power by killing off all his old business rivals one by one. They say he buried one man while he was still alive." Toasta shrugged. "I don't know if that's true. But, I'll tell you what I do know. No money moves in Jamaica without the Davidsons touching it first."

I listened to Toasta's words, but kept my eyes fixed on Dada. I already didn't like this guy. He sounded like a spoiled punk used to getting his way. I nodded, more determined than ever not to kiss this nigga's ass. I was willing to bet that young Dada had inherited every bad bone in his father's body.

Toasta gestured toward a man standing in the corner. He wore sunglasses that did little to hide the scar that ran the length of his face. His scowl only added to his deadly demeanor.

"That's Kutan. The Enforcer. He does all of Dada's dirty work. The nigga kill for fun."

I listened, my eyes scanning the room, taking in the scene.

Dada was in a conversation with Raddy Rich, the same performer who had wowed the crowd a little while ago. Dada stared at Raddy Rich sinisterly. He smoked a fat joint, and blew the smoke through his teeth completely covered in sparkling gold fronts.

Me and Toasta watched from the side as Dada pulled out a fat brick of dollar bills and slid it across the table toward Raddy Rich.

"You're officially part of the Dada Posse now." Dada was smiling. But, somehow he still managed to look sinister.

Raddy Rich wasn't smiling at all. "All respect. But, I don't know about—"

"No man refuses Don Dada! Mi let you wear your gold, and your fancy clothes. No charge. No one harass you, right?"

Raddy Rich shook his head.

Dada said, "Protection has a cost. Now, taxes due. You will win this competition for the posse. Take the money. Make your life easy. We can do this nice, and gentlemanly. Or not so, brethren. Your choice. Dance for the Posse or never dance again. Pretty easy decision, right?"

That smile was back on Dada's face again, even more evil than before.

Raddy Rich stared down at his hands for a while. I could see the decision weighing on him before he accepted that there was really no choice at all.

"Yes, sir. Dada Posse."

"For life!" Dada raised his bottle of champagne in a toast. He waved Raddy Rich away like he was dismissed, then motioned me and Toasta over. We walked through the barricade of goons. Toasta was a big man. But I noticed that even he walked cautiously through the maze of men. A couple of them stared us down extra hard. But, Dada spoke up.

"Nah, man. Dem cool. The Selectah! All Star Toasta! Mi brethren. Wha' g'wan?"

Four gorgeous girls surrounded Dada and his crew. Their clothes were skimpy, and their bodies were tight.

"Respect, Mr. Dada. And blessings." Toasta greeted Dada with the utmost respect.

Dada just sat there and kept smoking his joint. His whole demeanor was very ominous and calm. He was so laid-back that I had to resist the urge to slap the shit out of him. Dudes like this wouldn't last a day in Brooklyn. Born with a silver spoon in his mouth, but out here fronting like a gangsta. I sized him up, but kept my poker face on. After all, I wanted to do business with this fake ass nigga. For now.

"What can I do for ya?" He blew the smoke in Toasta's face as he asked it.

"Well, Mr. Dada—"

"Call me Don." He smirked a little.

Toasta nodded. "Don—"

"Don Dada." His smile widened.

Toasta was looking less amused. "Don Dada. This is my cousin Tarzan, from Brooklyn."

I extended my hand to shake Dada's. But, he didn't budge.

"So?" Dada puffed on his joint, and left me hanging.

I withdrew my hand. My pride was wounded, but I somehow willed myself not to bust this cracker's jaw wide open.

Toasta cleared his throat. "So . . . Tarzan is looking to get hooked up with some Grade A ganja. About five thousand American."

Dada looked at me. He wore shades, despite the fact that it was the middle of the night in a packed ass dancehall. He looked at me like I was interviewing for a job as the help. He looked down at my Timbs and smirked.

"Tarzan," he said, finally. "Monkey man."

His boys laughed, and the tension rose. Toasta tensed up and looked at me.

Dada sucked his teeth. "Mi nah interested."

I spoke for the first time since we sat down. "Look, man. I got the cash right here." I reached to pull out my cash and slap the wad on the table, and the goons reacted instantly. They moved in like the secret service, swarming the table with their hands on their weapons. I held my own hands up in surrender.

Dada sat there calmly.

"Mi say mi nah interested."

He pulled out the prettiest gun I had ever seen—gold with a pearl handle.

My heart thundered in my chest. I knew that my life was hanging in the balance at that moment.

Toasta held his hands up in surrender. "No disrespect, Don Dada. I apologize for insulting you."

Dada turned and kissed the chocolate thottie sitting next to him. He waved us away without another word. Toasta walked off, and nudged me toward the door. I didn't budge. I stood my ground, my pride wounded. I wanted to kill this arrogant clown. I knew I was outnumbered, and that the possibility of me surviving a battle with Dada was slim to none. But, I didn't care. I felt rage coursing through my veins.

Then, I felt a soft hand encircle mine and I turned to see Maya standing there.

"Come downstairs with me," she said. Her voice was so sweet, and so welcome at that moment. She led me back down to the dance floor. I saw her roll her eyes in Dada's direction as we left.

A slow, melodic reggae song was playing now. Maya wrapped my arms around her waist, lightly, and swayed to the rhythm.

"So, ya trying to get killed your first day here?"

"Nah. Not at all. What you mean?"

"Young Don Dada. That's what I mean."

I shook my head. "No. We were just discussing some potential business opportunities."

"Trust. Dada is not someone you wan' do business with."

"Why? Because he has tattoos and gold teeth? You shouldn't judge a book by its cover, Maya. He's probably a scared little boy underneath all that costume."

Maya shook her head. "It's not a joke, Tarzan. That man kill for fun. I know him. Stay away from him. Ya don't wan' that kind of attention."

I smiled, flattered by her obvious concern for my safety. "Well what kind of attention do I want?"

She smiled. "This kind of attention." She grinded and winded all over me. I tried to handle it a little better this time.

"Just relax, and follow me," she said.

I got the hang of it. I reminded myself that this wasn't Brooklyn, and that none of my boys were watching and laughing. I let myself go, and let loose in the moment with Maya. Soon our dancing was natural. It felt sexy and sensual.

Maya breathed heavily on the inside of my neck. We were both sweaty, our bodies pressed closely as the music swelled all around us. I leaned in for a kiss.

Maya stopped me, her fingers on my lips.

"No," she said. "Just dancing."

I was a little embarrassed, but I manned up. I kept dancing with her, willing to take whatever I could to keep her in my arms. She relaxed. It was clear to me that she was running the show. It was a nice change of pace. Maya had my full attention.

So much that I didn't notice Dada watching us from the balcony. Thankfully, Toasta had my back from the dee-jay booth. So did Casanova at the bar. They both watched as Dada shook his head, his eyes focused on me and Maya dancing together. He smoked his joint, and motioned to a group of men standing near me on the dance floor.

"Dada Posse!" he yelled.

Raddy Rich, now wearing the DADA POSSE jacket, rushed the floor with the rest of the dance crew. They stepped up, pushing me and Maya back to make room for their routine.

The crowd gathered around, cheering them on, as Maya and I got shoved apart.

I looked up then and saw Dada. His face was twisted into that evil grin I hated. I knew this guy was gonna be a fucking problem.

RUDE AWAKENING

Toast and I drove Maya home after we left the dance-hall. Maya and I held hands as I walked her to the door of her father's house. I was already smitten by the pretty young thing, and I wanted to hold on to her hand for as long as I could.

Her father, the bishop, was waiting up for Maya when we got there. He came to the door, and I could immediately see where Maya had inherited her regal qualities from. The bishop stood with his shoulders squared, spine straight, and neck extended. It gave the appearance that he was literally looking down his nose at me. I didn't have much experience with fathers. None of the girls in my past had had the luxury of their father's presence. Neither had I, for that matter. So, I wasn't really sure how to approach this dude.

He scowled at me as we approached. It looked like he was in no mood for introductions. Nervously, Maya told him my name anyway.

"Tarzan is Toasta's cousin."

Bishop grunted. He shook my hand a lot harder than he had to, mumbled something in an accent thicker than I had ever heard, then shuffled back inside the house with a scowl on his face. Maya didn't hang around for long before she followed her father inside, leaving me standing there in the dark.

I went back to Aunt Cheryl's and crashed. I woke up the next morning after a few hours' sleep. I was exhausted after the night I had. I had a crazy hangover. I sat on the edge of the bed in my boxers only. The heat felt like a heavy blanket that I couldn't escape. Toasta was snoring like a wild animal on the top bunk. I remembered him struggling to get his big ass up there last night. I laughed, and sat up. At that moment, Aunt Cheryl busted in the room.

"Allester! Tarzan!"

She was yelling like she was calling us across the yard. Instead, she was standing like a foot away, screaming in Toasta's ear.

"Get yourselves up now and eat!"

Toasta popped up, startled by the shrill sound of his mama's voice.

"Mommy, okay! I'm not fourteen years old anymore."

"Shut up! You act like it. Don't draw mi tongue! I want you both out of 'ere and off to work in twenty minutes!"

"All right!" Toasta sucked his teeth so hard that I was worried Aunt Cheryl might slap the shit out of him.

"Raise your talk at me again and nah see if ya never walk again!" She stormed out of the room, cursing under her breath. I could smell the food she was cooking, and it was enough to sober me up. I left Toasta and followed my aunt into the kitchen.

By the time Toasta dragged his ass to the bathroom and washed up, got dressed, and sat down to eat, I was ready to go.

We got to Uncle Screechie's restaurant and he worked me like a slave. Somehow, Toasta's lazy ass managed to avoid work most of the time. But, I was putting in work! It was exhausting. Uncle Screechie was a slave driver on the low.

I brought some garbage out back and got distracted by the water in the distance. I had a joint in my pocket, so I pulled it out and lit it. I let the sensation of the weed relax me, and I breathed in the tropical air. I wandered down close to the shoreline, and saw Plastic Man. He was a wanderer, always dressed in a dingy, oversized T-shirt, tattered shorts, and an old smelly suit jacket. He was carrying an old boom box in his shopping cart, pumping a dancehall track and dancing for the tourists and patrons along the shore. He was surprisingly flexible, and he impressed his audience with his moves and his theatrical flair. I watched as the tourists danced to his rhythm. The women winded their waists seductively, their hair blowing in the wind. It looked erotic from where I stood. I was reminded again of the pirates Toasta had told me about. Even the breeze that blew around me had a sensual feel to it.

Still smoking my joint, I stood off in the distance throwing rocks at the water, trying to see if I could land one. I had a lot on my mind. Mainly, how the hell I was going to get my hustle on without the assistance of Dada's bitch ass.

I heard Toasta approach me from behind.

"Man, if Uncle Screechie catches you out here bullshitting, he's gonna be on you."

"I'm not worried about Uncle Screechie." I looked at

Toasta seriously. "What I'm worried about is your connect."
I shook my head, thinking about Dada and how rude he
had been at The Jungle. "I guess that relationship ain't what
you thought it was."

Toast sighed. "It was just a bad night for young Dada.
Small tings." Toasta lit a joint of his own.

"So now what?"

"I got a better plan." Toasta had a mischievous grin on
his face.

"You always got a better plan. What is it?"

"I got a farmer up in the mountains. Boss man. He is
the source. Straight, raw, and uncut. That good shit from
the ground." He took another puff.

I looked at him, skeptically. "So you want me to start my
operation with a farmer, Toast?"

He nodded. "That's the best way, man. I should have
went that route in the first place. You get the greatest quality without having to deal with all the street politics. No
dons. No territories. No percentages. Just all profit."

"All right, fam. If you lay it out, I'll play it out. I'm following your lead."

He nodded again. "He's way up in the mountains,
though. Take a long time to get there."

I shrugged. "I got nothing but time."

"Bet. We'll go as soon as you get off work." He said it
with a smirk.

I frowned. "Yo, I don't really work here." This whole
thing was supposed to be a front. Not a real job.

"That's not what Uncle Screechie thinks."

At that moment, Uncle Screechie appeared out of nowhere, holding two big bags of trash.

"Tarzan! Work! Di trash is calling. It nah take out itself!"

I sucked my teeth, while Toasta stood there laughing. I started walking back toward Uncle Screechie, and Toasta followed. I took the trash out, cursing as the fish guts spilled out of the bag and all over me. I tried to ignore my cousin snickering on the sidelines. I tried to remind myself that tonight we were going to meet the plug.

I finished putting the trash out, and did my best to cover the stench of the fish on my clothes. Finally, it was three o'clock, and I was off from work. We headed toward Toasta's car. I had something on my mind.

"Toast, let me ask you something."

"Nope. I got a job. I don't do trash. You're on your own."

"Nah. I was gonna ask you . . . do you think Maya was digging me last night, or just dancing?"

He laughed. "Uh-huh. Someone got bit by the Maya bug. Be careful, man. That bite can spread and you will be scratching that itch until it bleeds!"

I frowned. "What? I don't even know what the hell you're talking about. Just give me her number and shut up."

We got in the car, and Toasta rolled all of the windows all the way down. He squeezed his nose closed. He started the car, grumbling, with his head practically out the driver's side window.

"Bumba clot! You stink, nigga!" He gasped for air.

"Kiss my ass, Toast! You the one that set me up with this wack ass job with Uncle Screechie! I shouldn't even be doing this shit!" I did stink, there was no question. And now we had to sit there smelling it while we drove way up in the mountains to see the farmer. I wanted out of these clothes.

"I didn't know he was gonna have you knee deep in fish shit!"

We rode in silence for a while. Toasta continued to complain, but I ignored him after a few minutes.

"You never answered my question about Maya," I said. "You think she feeling me or nah?"

He shook his head. "Maya is in love with dancehall. That's her only lover. She lives and breathes the dance. When she's not helping her father and Peta Gaye, she's practicing her moves. When she's not at home with her family, she's in the dancehall tearing up the floor. That's her passion. You want to get next to her, you better learn how to move!"

I laughed. "You know real niggas don't dance, Toast."

"I thought that way when I first came back here from Brooklyn. But, here the dancehall is where di rude boys rule. Not on the street corners. To be king of the dancehall is to be di top dog!"

I thought about it. I could dance. Still, I couldn't imagine myself bumping and grinding out there like some R&B dude or stripper or some shit. One thing was certain, though. I hadn't stopped thinking about Maya since I watched her hypnotic hips sway across the threshold of her father's house last night.

"You stink for real, dog." Toasta said it with all sincerity.

"How much further up this damn mountain do we have to go? We've been in this car for over an hour."

"Trust me." He shook his head, grimacing. "I'm ready to get out of here with your funky ass, too. We're about to pull up."

THE FARMER

I looked around at the mountainside, and I was speechless. The whole scene was beautiful. Lush green fields as far as the eye could see. The breathtaking view of Kingston miles below. It felt so peaceful and serene. I climbed out of the car, and lost myself for a second taking in the view. It was amazing.

"Here come Farmer." Toasta nodded toward an elderly man approaching from the distance. He had deep black skin that gleamed in the sunshine. He wore a tank top, some baggy pants, and a straw hat. He had a long beard, and he approached us chewing on some type of stick. His eyes were low and glassy. It was clear he was a Rasta that was at one with nature.

"Wha' g'wan, Farmer?" Toasta called out, smiling. He looked at me and whispered, "You stay here. You might mess up the vibe with your stinky ass." He walked to meet Farmer.

I smelled my shirt, and winced. I did smell terrible.

Toasta went off a short distance and spoke with the dark

and mellow stranger. After a few minutes he motioned me over.

"Farmer, this is my cousin Tarzan."

The farmer smiled. "Ah. The king of the jungle. Blessings, brotha."

We shook hands.

"Excuse the smell," I apologized.

"He's been working seafood at Uncle Screechie's," Toasta explained.

Farmer chuckled. "All mi smell is the goodness of Jah's greatest gift. Ganja."

I agreed. "It does smell pretty good out here. I didn't catch your name, sir."

He smirked. "They call me the farmer."

I waited.

"That's all ya need to know," he said.

I nodded. That made sense in his line of business. Toasta had explained to me that, contrary to popular belief, here in Jamaica marijuana wasn't really legal. So, when you operate one of the largest ganja farms on the island, it's best to be inconspicuous.

"As I was telling you, you can trust Tarzan the same way you trust me, brethren. You have mi word. This is family."

Farmer nodded. "Toasta tell mi you lookin' for luggage for vacation."

I was confused for a second. I glanced at my cousin and he nodded.

"Yeah," I said.

"How much you want?"

"I got five grand to start."

"Five grand U.S.?" His voice went up an octave. I understood it. Five grand in U.S. dollars was more than half a million Jamaican dollars. I was looking for a whole hell of a lot of weed.

I nodded.

"That's a lot of luggage for one man."

"It's gonna be a long vacation."

He smiled and his pearly whites sparkled in the sunshine. Finally, he nodded. "Give me a day to round up the particulars. Soon come."

"Okay."

"Mi need the money now, though."

I frowned. Farmer had me fucked up. I wasn't one of these naive young Jamaican boys running around trusting some mountain man I never met before. I looked at Toasta like this nigga was crazy. "Toasta, that shit goes against everything I learned in the streets."

Toasta nodded. "But, that was on the streets of New York, Tarzan. Things operate differently here."

I shook my head, unsure.

"I vouch for Farmer. You can trust him."

I stared at him for a long time. Farmer waited. Toasta nodded at me, encouragingly.

"A'ight." I reluctantly handed over the fat roll of hundreds. It was everything I had.

Farmer took it, tucked it into his pocket, and nodded.

"Come again in t'ree days' time, and we move fo'ward. Mi also provide services at the dock so no badmans or police can interfere. We operate very low key. Keeps a healthy business going. Ya understand?"

I did. I listened while Farmer outlined his operation. He

told me about the men he had all over Kingston. His team sounded organized and efficient. He spoke of how they moved through uptown and the lower territories. I felt more at ease as I listened to him. Handing over all my money didn't seem like such a bad move now. From the sound of it, Farmer was running one of the most sophisticated and notorious marijuana-trafficking operations in town.

We left, and took the long drive back to Hellshire. I felt a crazy mix of adrenaline and anxiety. I was excited, but fearful at the same time. The next few days would be tough to get through. I couldn't wait to get my hands on the product, and get money!

When we finally got back to town, Toasta pulled his old rusty Beamer up to the house he used to share with Peta Gaye. Today, the place was in complete chaos. The kids were crying, we could hear the sound of glass breaking, and above the noise of it all, Peta Gaye was yelling.

"Ya Daddy no help! He wan' run di street trying to be a badman deejay!"

I glanced at the house and realized that Peta Gaye was staring directly at us while she said it. Aware that her husband was within earshot, she yelled even louder.

"What type o' deejay makes no money? I cook, clean, and do every ting! Mi slave in this hellhole and look after the pickney! And what does mi husband do? Eh?"

Reluctantly, Toasta climbed out of the car and I followed. As we slowly walked toward the house, dreading the confrontation, Maya approached carrying an empty basket. She stopped when she saw me.

"Hey," I said. "Where ya off to?" My attempt at a Jamaican accent fell flat, and she laughed.

"On mi way to the market." She flashed me a pretty smile and walked off.

I looked at Toasta, ready to tell him that I was leaving with Maya. But, he already knew what was up.

"Let me go inside here and handle this madness. You go catch up to ya likkle girlfriend."

He was teasing me, but I didn't care. I trotted off to catch up with the woman who had my full attention.

SWEET THING

As I got closer to her, I grabbed a handful of my shirt and sniffed it. I still smelled like old trash and fish shit. I snatched my shirt off and threw it away, just as I caught up to Maya.

She looked at me with her eyes wide. "Whappem to ya shirt?"

"Long story," I said. "Anyway, I thought you would want to see the six-pack abs." I flexed my muscles for her.

Maya smiled. "Please! I just don't wan' ya likkle pickney chest to catch cold."

I pretended to be offended and she laughed. She was trying to front like she didn't appreciate the view. But, I noticed her checking out my body, admiring my tattoos.

"You mind if I come with you to the market?"

She shrugged, and I walked alongside her. The island seemed even more beautiful than usual while I was walking with her. It seemed like the colors, the scents and sounds all came alive.

"Your sister seemed pretty upset back there," I said.

"Mi sista too hot at everyone 'cause Toasta nah live right."

I frowned. "What you mean? Toast is a good dude."

She sucked her teeth. "Him head in di clouds. Always big talk and dreams about making music in di States and selling millions of records. But him can't take care of him babies. Mi nah like a dreamer. Him a buguyaga."

I stopped walking. I was from Brooklyn, but my mother was born and raised on this island. I knew the dialect well enough to know that Maya had just called my cousin a bum.

"Hey!"

I saw remorse flash across her face. She stopped walking and apologized.

"That wasn't nice. I'm sorry."

We started walking again.

"Now that I'm here, things are gonna turn around for Toasta. You'll see."

She looked at me. "Mmm. Ya don't say."

"I'm for real. I'm not a dreamer. I stay woke, and I work shit out. I'm a hustler. If there's something I want, I go and get it."

"Well, what is that you want?"

I looked at her, wondering if she knew that right now the answer was her.

"I want to make all the people that I love happy."

We arrived at the market. It was completely different from the supermarkets back in Brooklyn. Here, there were beautiful, fresh, colorful fruits and vegetables as far as the eye could see. A few elderly women managed each station as Maya and I blended in with the locals walking around filling their baskets.

Maya grabbed a few mangoes and placed them in her basket. I took it from her, and carried it for her the rest of our time there.

"Look, Maya." I spoke up after a few minutes of shopping in silence. "The other night at the dancehall, I saw how you was digging me."

She laughed, loudly. "Mi nah know what ya talk 'bout, Tarzan. It was just a dance. Nothing more than that."

I felt disappointed. "So you dance with all the guys like that?"

"Yes, sir!"

"For real?"

She nodded. "And most of dem can actually handle it." She walked ahead of me.

"Wait! I could handle it."

She looked back over her shoulder and shot me a look that said, *Yeah, right.*

I caught up to her. "Okay," I admitted. "Maybe I couldn't handle it last night. But, I want to handle it. I was getting the hang of it. I want to learn how to dance. Can you teach me?"

She looked at me, skeptically. "Ya fah real? Ya wan' learn?"

"I'm for real," I said.

"When?" Her eyes were dancing. I could tell she was excited. The thought of that excited me, too.

I stepped closer to her. "Right now."

We were finished at the market within minutes.

TEACHER'S PET

She took me to a church and pulled me inside. The sun had set, and the place was dark and still. Maya pulled me down the back corridor of the cathedral, and checked to make sure that the coast was clear. Quietly, she began to light candles in the back room.

A mirror and about a dozen blazing candles were our only companions in the room. It felt simultaneously romantic and spooky.

"Yo, you bringing me to a vacant church to teach me how to dance? That's a little strange."

"Dis is mi father's church. It's where I always rehearse. The only place with a mirror large enough to practice in." She lit another candle. "This is my sanctuary in more ways than one. It's the only place where I feel truly safe."

I was still confused. "So . . . we gonna be winding and grinding in the Lord's house?"

She chuckled. "You sound like my father. I say, 'God sees us no matter where we are. So why hide it?' Besides,

God loves dancehall." She smiled at me. "It's just dancing, remember?"

She turned on a small radio in the corner. A sexy dance-hall track by Sean Paul began to play.

She faced me, grabbed my hands, and placed them on her hips. Then she spun around and my hands were magically on her backside.

For the briefest moment, I started to pull back, aware that we were in a church. But, then I snapped out of it and realized that this was the chance of a lifetime. I kept my hands firmly in place as she started to slowly wind her hips against me.

"All ya have to do is go with the vibe. Feel di rhythm. Gently."

Her voice was soft, and mellow. I did as she told me, and went with the vibe.

"See?" she said. "You naturally have it. Jamaicans move to a different rhythm. It's the upbeat."

She popped her backside to the upbeat she was speaking of. I followed, determined to keep up this time.

She encouraged me. "There ya go! Ya got it."

She swung her hips even more now.

"You pick up quickly. It's all swagger and sexiness."

"Well, I definitely got that."

"Oh really?" She had a mischievous expression on her face. "Well, can ya go low?"

She dropped it low to the ground and I followed. I was handling that thing.

"Okay," she said, giggling. "I see!"

She dipped it even lower. I tried to do the same, but fell back on my ass instead. I was pissed.

Maya laughed. "You'll get the hang of it. Patience, Tarzan."

She looked so beautiful in the sunlight reflecting through the church's stained glass windows. The heat between us was electric. A warm breeze blew in through the open window, tickling my skin and making my senses come alive. I felt a wave of spiritual energy overtake me. It was unlike anything I had ever experienced before. I felt inhabited by a spirit that was so pure and so erotic at the same time. I lost all control. I flipped her over so that she was lying on her back beneath me on the floor. I straddled her and we were face-to-face. The sexual tension between us was thick enough to slice. I could feel it, and I was sure that she could, too.

I couldn't help myself. I leaned in and kissed her passionately. She seemed reluctant at first. But, finally, she went with it. She kissed me back with so much intensity that I groaned, hungry for her. Although we were no longer dancing, there was still a rhythm to our kiss. Everything with Maya felt natural, and unforced. I lost myself in the rapture of the moment. It felt like a dream, and I didn't want to wake up.

I slowly peeled her shirt off, revealing her pretty bra. I was so hard that it almost hurt. I moved in to kiss her skin. Then, Maya pulled back.

"Wait . . ."

I sighed. The spell had been broken. It occurred to me that this was definitely not the place for this.

"My bad," I said. "You're right. Not in your father's church."

"Nah. Mi nah care about that."

"Word?" I looked at her, surprised.

"I believe there's nothing to hide from God."

I nodded. That made sense.

"It's just . . . mi nah . . ." She looked away, embarrassed.

"You're a virgin?"

She nodded yes.

I drew back in shock. "Wait. All of that winding and grinding you do when you dance and you've never had sex?"

She shook her head.

"Wow. You could've fooled me. You move like a veteran."

"Mi tell ya before. It's just dancing. I consider mi'self a queen. A man will have to be my king to enter the castle."

I laughed. "Really?"

She was serious. "One day I may meet a king. But, until I do, mi nah ready."

I was impressed. "I guess I gotta respect that."

She looked at me, her eyes searching me. "So you finish with your dance lessons now that ya nah getting the pum?"

I shook my head. "Nah. I still want to dance. I told you, I want to learn. So we can dance all night." I stood up.

She looked at me, wide-eyed. "Really? You just want to dance?"

"Just dance. I want to master this."

She stared at me in silence for a few moments. I could tell she was pondering something.

"If you want to really master this, you gotta go all the way. The realness. The raw, dutty yard!"

"Okay," I said. "Let's go."

She smiled. "Okay. Let me talk to a couple of people. Mi have plans for you, Tarzan."

I smiled. "I like the sound of that."

THE COME UP

I had a lot on my mind while the next couple of days ticked by. First off, Maya consumed my thoughts. The feeling of her body pressed against mine; the taste of her mouth and her skin. I caught myself daydreaming about her more than once. My mind was also preoccupied with thoughts of Farmer. I worried that he might play me, take all my money and run. I had given him a whole lot of money. I was starting to have doubts about whether Toasta knew this nigga as well as he thought he did.

I kept busy with my work at Uncle Screechie's, and I even spent some time helping Aunt Cheryl in her garden. As gruff as she was, she had a warm spirit. While we tended the soil, she shared her concerns about her son. Just like my mother, she wanted the best for her child. She worried about him down at the dancehall where life and death were separated by a very thin line. I assured her that Toasta was safe. Especially now that I was in town. I promised to have his back and to keep my eyes open.

I called home and let my mama know that I was okay. That I had found a job, and I was staying out of trouble and helping Aunt Cheryl. She wasn't happy that I had sent my brother back home with an envelope full of cash and no explanation. She was even more upset that I had left town without telling her first. But she seemed relieved to hear that I had gotten into a routine on the island where she was born and raised. It comforted her to know that I was safe with family. Trent let me know that, despite her protests, she had put the money to good use and they were all right. That set my mind at ease while I waited for my hustle to start.

In the evenings, Toasta and I headed out to the dancehall. I loved it there, and found myself looking forward to arriving each night. The music became a part of me. Back in Brooklyn, I had never spent much time listening to the lyrics of many reggae songs I had heard over the years. But now I was truly hearing the songs for the first time, discovering a love for the music that was new to me. Watching the dancers each night, I came to understand that the rhythm and the movement were part of the culture. I grew up thinking that dancing was something corny dudes did in the background of music videos and at goofy neighborhood talent shows. But, this was different. I started to understand why Toasta had hyped up this lifestyle so much while I was away. It felt like we were on the verge of something big that was bubbling just below the surface. He was deejaying at the hottest dancehall club in Kingston. Night after night I was there, soaking it all up.

I was also watching Maya. I was soaking up all the little nuances of her. The way that she bit her lip when she danced. The way her arms moved, the sway of her neck.

She became a bit of an obsession for me. Each night, she was at The Jungle with her girls, battling rival dance crews for the number one spot. I watched her from the sidelines, still trying to get up the nerve to join her on the dance floor. My experience had taught me that she was not an easy one to handle in private. I wasn't sure that I could hold it together in front of a crowd. For now, I was content to be her captive audience. I loved to watch her move. From my vantage point, she was the sexiest woman in all of Kingston.

On the third day Farmer proved to be a man of his word. Toasta and I skipped work at Uncle Screechie's and headed up the mountainside once more. Farmer hit us off with a ton of weed, and we sat down with him and set up our whole operation. Farmer delivered my "luggage," literally. His men arrived with several large suitcases packed with marijuana. The bricks of weed were Saran-wrapped and zipped into various articles of clothing inside.

Farmer explained the way things worked down at the docks. He gave us the cost of doing business there, with cruise ships coming in daily and certain customs agents willing to look the other way for the right price. I contacted Kareem back in Brooklyn, and urged him to book the next flight to Kingston. Now was the time to put my plan in motion. If everything went smoothly, we were all about to make a whole lot of money.

Toasta and I split the weed between Aunt Cheryl's house and the home he shared with Peta Gaye. Neither woman knew what we were up to. Otherwise, there would have been hell to pay. We moved quietly, and acted as if nothing had changed. We continued working at Uncle Screechie's, coming and going like nothing was different.

Until Farmer helped us assemble our crew; we had a whole lot of weed and only the two of us to move it. Toasta assured me that we could make a killing at The Jungle each night. We could also sell it to the tourists and patrons at Uncle Screechie's restaurant. But, that would only begin to put a dent in the amount of work we had. I needed a team.

As if in answer to my prayers, Maya met me at Uncle Screechie's restaurant when I was done with my shift that Friday.

"You ready for the next part of ya lesson?" She rubbed her hands together, excitedly.

I took off my work shirt. "Yeah. Let's go."

She took me to a part of town I wasn't familiar with. We walked through a maze of empty buildings to an old abandoned warehouse. It was full of broken-down cars and scraps of metal. I saw a group of thugged-out yard boys chilling in the back. A couple of them were leaning on the cars, smoking weed and drinking liquor straight from the bottle.

Two of the guys drew weapons the second they spotted us. One held a gun, the other a machete. I stopped in my tracks, but Maya laughed and kept right on walking in their direction.

"Simmer down, boys. Mi tol' ya mi was comin'."

The grimaces were instantly replaced with smiles when they realized it was Maya.

The guy holding the machete kept grilling me, though. He wasn't grinning at all. Just staring me down like he wanted beef.

Maya sensed the tension.

"Killa Bean, meet Tarzan. As mi tell you, di man from foreign. So for me, be nice. Make him feel at home."

She looked at me. "These guys are the best underground crew in all of Jamaica."

Killa Bean looked me over, skeptically. He grunted a bit. Kicked the ground. I couldn't tell what he was thinking. He looked at me again, long and hard. "Him a dancer? Can him move?"

Maya smiled. "A likkle bit. But we g'wan fix that."

I nodded. "Yeah. I'm decent. But, y'all can help me get good."

Killa Bean shook his head. "Dancehall is never good." He seemed offended. Speaking in his thick accent, he addressed his boys and they shared a laugh at my expense. "We always bad."

"That's right. Blood, sweat, and tears. Every day. We work fast and hard," Maya said.

"Dis nah for play. We pull from di heart. Moves represent our yard, our soil. Dis real ting!" Killa Bean used his machete to punctuate his words. He took this shit seriously, it was clear.

I looked at Maya. She wore a tank top and a pair of tiny shorts, accentuating every curve to perfection. I would have followed her to the ends of the earth.

"Well, then let's go," I said. "I'm ready."

For the first time since meeting me, Killa Bean smiled at me. "Come on, man. Let mi school ya."

His crew gathered around and they began to show me a few moves. We started with the basics. They taught me the core moves and footwork to a routine they were putting together. I picked them up quickly. I had always been light on my feet. Back in Brooklyn, I had used that skill to maneuver down fire escapes with stolen goods. Now I was using it to dance, picking up the steps with ease. Killa watched, grunting his approval. The dancehall tracks echoed off the walls of the warehouse as we danced. Maya stood on the sidelines, pleased that the All Star Blazers had accepted me into the fold. She watched me dance, and there were a few times when I thought I caught her staring a little longer than usual. By the time the sun began to set, I was drenched in sweat, and had mastered several moves I never thought I could do.

I leaned against a wall, exhausted. Killa Bean came over and shook my hand. We locked eyes and he gave me a nod.

"Good work, Tarzan."

I thanked him. "You and your crew," I said, hesitantly. "Do y'all need work? I got some luggage I might need some help moving."

Killa Bean looked at me. "Hell yeah we need work. What kind of luggage ya have?"

I glanced over my shoulder to be sure that Maya wasn't listening. She was on the other end of the warehouse practicing a handstand move with one of Killa's crew members. I turned back to Killa and laid it out. I told him what I had and mapped out my plan. When I finished, he was smiling wider now, from ear to ear.

"Tarzan, mi boy. Welcome to di crew!"

Now, I had a team. That was just what I needed.

Killa became my main man on the streets. He knew Kingston the way a mouse knows the framework of the house he lives in. With his help, we doubled our money—first selling hand to hand throughout Kingston, then becoming the middlemen for crews on the city's outskirts. Farmer had some of the best marijuana in Jamaica, and now we had the manpower to move it.

Over the next several weeks, my whole life changed. I spent less and less time at Uncle Screechie's. My days were spent hustling marijuana with Killa and his crew, and rehearsing dance routines with Killa and his crew. We formed a bond that was unbreakable. Killa and his boys became my Jamaican brethren, as close to me as my niggas back in Brooklyn. For the first time in my life, I felt like I was truly a part of something. This was something way bigger than me. This was a culture. A world that had accepted me, and that I had embraced as a new family. We put work into our dancing and in the streets. We were making stacks of money, and Killa and the crew appreciated me for coming to the island and turning their lives around. Little did they know, they had done the same for me. Dancehall was my life.

We were all driving now. Toasta got himself a brand-new Beamer, while I opted for a beautiful motorcycle I nicknamed "Dutty." Killa and the crew got cars and bikes of their own. But, more importantly, we were all able to handle our responsibilities as men. I sent money home to my mother and Toasta helped Aunt Cheryl fix up her place. He moved back in with Peta Gaye and I got a humble little place nearby. Things were better than ever.

Farmer kept the weed coming, and Kareem made his first voyage to Kingston to pick up a suitcase. He stayed for a couple of days, taking a little time to soak up the dancehall scene and the new life I was living in the tropics. He was apprehensive at first, just like I had been. But, when he saw it for himself, and witnessed the brand-new life I had created for myself, he was impressed. We reminisced on the old days in Brooklyn, and talked about our plans to get a whole lot of money together in the months to come. When it was time for him to leave, he took a cruise from the docks of Jamaica back to the shores of Miami with a suitcase full of weed. At both ends of the trip, Farmer's connects met Kareem at the port and made sure that he got through all right. In Miami, one of his boys picked him up and together they drove for three days back to New York. Kareem was now on the streets of Brooklyn with some sticky green straight from the shores of Kingston. He was making money, we were making money, and life was good.

Maya and I were getting closer, too. In between my rehearsals with Killa and the crew and my grind on the streets of Kingston, I managed to carve out time for her. I would stop by the church when I knew she was rehearsing and watch her. She seemed to enjoy having my attention as much as I liked giving it to her. Often we danced together in the solitude of the empty church, and it felt like we were alone in the world. Those were some of the happiest moments of my life.

She had started to change her mind about my cousin. When we first met, she thought Toasta was a bum. But, over time she came to realize that he wasn't such a bad guy. He was just a man obsessed with achieving his dreams. As the money started rolling in, and Toasta began to provide for his family more consistently, Peta Gaye was smiling again. Toasta even gave money to Aunt Cheryl to help her fix her leaking roof. For once, it seemed that everyone was happy. It was almost too good to be true in my mind. Things never went very well for long. Not in my life.

Sure enough, Maya invited me to really sit down and meet her father, the bishop. She suggested that maybe he had been in a bad mood the first time. She was convinced that if he got to know me, he would like me just as much as she did. Needless to say, that didn't go as well as expected.

Bishop was a proud man. He had a calm voice, smooth dark skin, a bald head, and an air of importance. He was born in Ghana, and had moved to Jamaica to work for the embassy. He had met Maya's mother soon after his arrival in Jamaica, and they fell in love. When she died, he raised their daughters to have respect and Christian values. It hadn't been easy. Both girls were lovely, easy prey for the wolves lurking about. Understandably, Bishop was a protective father, viciously defending his daughters' honor.

Toasta was not the type of man he would have chosen for his eldest daughter, Peta Gaye. But, she had married him anyway. The headaches that ensued were what he used to warn Maya against making the same mistakes. Bishop wanted Maya to marry a righteous man. And it was clear from the second he laid eyes on me—still wearing my blue Yankees fitted cap and my Timberland boots—that I wasn't what he had in mind.

He shook my hand hard. "Tarzan." He looked me in the eyes. "Maya has told me a lot about you."

I smiled. "She speaks very highly of you, sir. Everyone does. I'm honored to meet with you."

He exhaled deeply, his focus solely on me. He seemed to be taking me all in, sizing me up. I stood there, undaunted.

I had nothing to hide. What you see is what you get with me. He looked at me with his eyes narrowed.

"Are you a Christian, Tarzan?"

I shrugged. "Not really," I answered, honestly. "From my experience, if there is a god, He don't seem to be paying attention to what's going on out here."

Maya cringed. Her father's frown deepened.

"So you are a godless man?" His voice was critical.

"I ain't say all that. I'm just saying . . . look . . . I'm keeping it real. I'm not the most religious nig—the most religious dude out here. It's like Santa Claus. Some people believe in him. Some people don't. I just don't believe in all that religion stuff. You feel me?"

Maya looked like she might cry. I knew I had fucked up.

"Mr. . . . what did you say your last name was, young man?"

"Brixton."

He nodded. "Mr. Brixton, I'm glad that Maya brought you here to meet me." He grinned. But even though the gesture seemed friendly, I could sense his annoyance. "Before you arrived here today, Maya had so many positive tings to say about you. I see now that she has been viewing you through rose-colored glasses."

"Daddy—"

"No, Maya. See, dis why I tell ya to stay away from that *dancehall*." He spoke the word with so much venom that even I frowned in contempt. "It's no place for a bishop's daughter. Dis boy is a sinner and a no-good Yankee man. Ya wan' end up like ya sister with five kids and nah pot fi piss in?" Bishop looked at me with disdain, and shook his head. "Maya, stay away from dancehall trash."

He walked back inside of his house, and I stood there—both deeply offended and full of regret.

"Maya, I didn't mean to—"

"Tarzan, go home. I need to smooth things over with mi father. I'll talk to you tomorrow."

She walked away and went inside the house. I stood there for a minute, wondering if I should try to explain myself a little better. But I was afraid I would only make it worse. I got on my motorcycle and headed back to my place.

On the way there, I thought about my conversation with the bishop. I had been honest. My mother had raised me to believe in God and heaven and hell and all that stuff. But, I wasn't really sure those things existed. I watched my mother work like a slave, saw her be kind to her neighbors and her friends. And now she was alone suffering from kidney failure. None of those friends were around. And I found it hard to imagine that a God who loved her would allow her to suffer like that. I thought about her prayers. All those prayers she was constantly saying. I hadn't seen one of those prayers answered in all these years.

My mother's troubles weren't my only reason for questioning the existence of an almighty being. Growing up on the streets of New York, I had witnessed some unthinkable things. I had seen young boys slain in the street. Watched their mothers wail at the funerals of those boys. I had seen women selling their bodies, drug addicts selling their souls, and children left alone to raise themselves. In prison, the horrors I observed had only been worse. I listened to grown men cry in their beds at night while the demons of mass incarceration closed in around them. With all that I had seen and had experienced for myself, it was tough to imagine that there was anyone out there listening to our desperate prayers.

I got to my small villa, parked my bike, and went inside. Nestled in the hills, the place was small but it was home. I got comfortable and set my gun down on the bedside table. I took a bunch of money out of my pocket and set it aside. Later, I would tuck it into my safe along with all the rest of the cash I had managed to save. The stacks in that safe were getting higher. I was happy. Everything was going according to plan. Except with Maya. I was afraid that I had messed things up with her for good.

I called home to speak to my mother. Weeks had passed since the last time I heard her voice. I knew that she alone could make me feel better and take my mind off my relationship problems.

She answered the phone, and I could hear the excitement in her voice instantly.

"Tarzan? Is that you?"

I laughed. "Yeah, Ma. It's me. How you doing?"

"Boy, I haven't heard from you in weeks! I would be doing fine if you would call more often."

"I'm sorry, Ma. I've been busy working down at Uncle Screechie's place."

She sucked her teeth. "Tarzan, don't even try it. I spoke to Screechie two days ago, and he said he hardly sees you these days. You're not working with him as much as you used to. You stop in there once or twice a week, and show your face for a few minutes."

I sighed. Damn Uncle Screechie!

"I don't know how you keep sending all this money up here. I don't like it, Tarzan."

I was rethinking my decision to call home. "Mama . . . I thought you said you needed the money. They got you on all that medicine. You hate it. At least that's what you told me. You like your holistic remedies. Your herbs and po-tions. You can't get all of that with insurance, can you?"

She hesitated. "No. But, I—"

"And, your rent was backed up. You're caught up now, right?"

"Yes, it's paid."

"And you have a little money set aside to send Trent to community college this fall?"

"Yes, son. I have everything I need, everything that Trenton needs. We have more than we need, as a matter of fact. But, I'm worried about you, Tarzan."

She was trying to give me a hard time. But, I could hear the relief in her voice. For the first time in a long time, she didn't have to duck the phone calls from credi-tors. She didn't have to come home from long dialysis ap-pointments to find eviction notices posted on her door anymore. My brother was on track to get the education he deserved. She had to be sleeping better at night. That's what I was doing all of this for. Or at least, that's what I told myself.

"Don't worry about me, Mama. I'm out here working with Uncle Screechie. I'm going to the dancehall club with Toasta and I'm having fun. I even met a girl."

"What?" I could hear the joy across the miles. "Ya nah ready for di island gals."

I laughed, and so did she. And, just like that, the mood was lightened.

"Is Trent there?" I asked.

She said that he was, and called him to the phone.

"What's up, Tarzan?" Trenton sounded older and more mature than the last time I spoke to him weeks ago.

"Hey. Did Kareem give you my message?"

"Yeah. I'll take care of it."

I had sent Kareem back to the States with some extra money, specifically for my brother. My instructions were for Trent to go shopping, get some sneakers, some gear. Flex, for the first time in his life.

"You spend so much time taking care of Mama. You know what I'm saying? You make sure she gets to her appointments. You work long hours and give her your whole paycheck sometimes in order to make ends meet. I know the sacrifices you have to make all the time. Most of it is my fault. By getting in trouble all the time, I leave you to hold it down. And you always do. So, I know your birthday is coming up. Make sure you go out and treat yourself good. Get yourself something nice."

"Yo, Tarzan. I appreciate that, brother. For real. Thank you."

It felt good to do that for him. For too long the roles had been reversed. Trent had been the man of the house while I was out breaking the law. Even now, I had left him back in Brooklyn alone to shoulder the weight of our mother's health problems. Kareem told me that things had died down with Charles. Apparently, Tameka had kicked him to the curb for the next baller. Now I was the furthest thing from his mind. Still, I knew my place was not in Brooklyn at the moment. I needed to be here. Jamaica had become a part of me in ways I had never expected.

I talked with my family for a little while longer, assured

them that I was taking care of myself. Then I took a nice, long shower and fell asleep across my bed with Marley singing softly through my little radio about redemption.

THE JUNGLE

Maya was pissed off, to say the least. Days went by without a word from her. I wasn't crazy enough to go back to the bishop's house again. Instead, I went looking for her at Toasta and Peta Gaye's house, only to be told that Maya didn't want to talk to me. She was shutting me out and there was nothing I could do about it.

I stayed busy, hanging out with Toasta, Killa Bean, and the crew. We created new moves and mastered our dance routines with relentless practicing. Killa was an ambitious choreographer. He liked to incorporate unexpected objects like beer bottles and lighters with aerosol cans to make torches. Our rehearsals were grueling and I had to really challenge myself to keep up. Truth be told, I was determined to do more than keep up. I wanted to exceed all expectations.

It took me a minute to realize that my motives had shifted over the course of the weeks I had spent in Kingston so far. My interest in dancehall had started out as an attempt to get in Maya's pants. If dancehall was the way to her heart, then dammit, that's the way I was going. But, then I got into the heart and soul of it and, to my surprise, started discovering layers of myself. I was glad the weed was selling and the money was rolling in. But, I was happiest in those moments when I danced with the All Star Blazers. I came alive out there. And, I watched my brothers do the same.

Killa Bean, especially, became an open book when he danced. All of his pain, his terror and power, his belief that he was invincible—it all spilled out when he danced. I learned that he had led a tough life in the heart of Kingston's historic unrest. War was something he had seen up close, and had lived to tell the story. He told that story with his feet, his arms, chest, and the sway of his neck as he moved. He taught me to do the same. I felt like I was learning from the best.

The "In the Dance" clash competition was coming up soon, and the grand prize was ten million Jamaican dollars. That was almost eighty grand in American currency. We were making good money in the streets. But, the All Star Blazers had every intention of winning that dance battle, and putting that prize money to good use. My plan was to take my share of the money and invest every penny into my cousin's music career. Toasta had gained an impressive following in the dancehall world. His mixtapes were selling more than ever, and he was requested to deejay at venues throughout Kingston. I believed that with the right push and the right people behind him, Toasta could go all the way.

But, it all depended on me and the All Star Blazers winning the dance clash. We had been practicing hard. It had taken discipline that I never knew I had to master some of the moves Killa Bean had come up with. Now, the dance had become a part of me. I understood that the steps were extensions of my swag. The way I popped my chest, moved my waist, shuffled my feet, tipped my hat, grabbed my belt—each movement was a demonstration of who I was. It all told my story. I was in love with the energy of it. My moves were bold, my facial expressions provocative. I intended to leave an impression tonight, as I took the floor with the All Star Blazers for the first time.

The energy felt higher than ever. I knew that was because I was dancing with Killa Bean and the crew for the first time in front of a crowd. I would be lying if I said that I wasn't nervous. I stood by the bar watching the scene. I peeped the fact that Dada was upstairs holding court with his usual goons. I saw Kutan, his enforcer, standing at the top of the railing with his gun visible in his shoulder holster. The air was thick with peril, adrenaline, and a raw, haunting energy. I tossed back so many shots of Hennessy at the bar that Casanova took notice.

"Nuttin' to be nervous about, brethren. Ya name is Tarzan. Ya rule The Jungle. Dis' shit come naturally."

I nodded, fronting that I had more confidence than I really felt. I started to say something else, but I stopped midsentence when I saw Maya getting ready to take the dance floor with her girls. She and her crew were dressed in denim booty shorts that left nothing to the imagination. In fact, the shorts looked more like denim thongs. I didn't appreciate seeing my lady with all her goodies on display like that. I stepped to her and let her know.

"Yo, what's this shit you got on?"

"Tarzan, mi nah time for ya nonsense, ya hear me?"

"I'm just saying . . . you need some more fabric on these outfits."

"I don't owe you an explanation. Mi not ya concern anymore."

I was crushed. But, before I could respond, Killa Bean was at my side.

"Let's go!" He nodded toward the crew behind him. "We're on."

It was time to hit the floor. I watched Maya walk away, and I followed Killa to the center of the floor. Toasta threw on our track.

"Gimme the Light" came on at full volume. The speakers vibrated with the pulse of the bass. Me and Killa Bean took our places at the front of the crew. The rest of the All Star Blazers were hype. This was it. We looked good. All of us were dressed in simple tank tops, jeans, and NY Yankees fitted caps. We wore dark sunglasses, despite the fact that it was the middle of the night. I knew our Yankee look would stand out. And that it would piss Dada off.

The Hennessy had kicked in and my adrenaline was racing. I wasn't nervous now. It was game time. All eyes were on us. We started our routine in the center of the dance floor.

Our moves were energetic, tight, and fluid. From behind my shades, I watched the crowd as I danced. All eyes were on us. We held beer bottles in our left hands, waving them like torches while we danced. We flipped the bottles to the rhythm of the drum beat, sending them spinning toward the sky, and caught them in midair. The crowd went crazy.

We kept going and it was just like Killa Bean had described. Each move illustrated our swagger, and it felt effortless. The All Star Blazers were bosses, and our movements out on that dance floor left no doubt about it. The women were screaming for us, and everyone had to give us love. Toasta was hype, jumping around in the deejay booth. The only ones standing still were Dada and his bitch ass crew up in his little fake VIP section. We nailed the final steps as the song ended. The crowd was cheering and yelling, their hands in the air. It was official. I was part of the dancehall family, and I had never felt more at home in my life.

My boys and I celebrated as Toasta bigged us up on the mic.

"All Star Blazers! Big up! We tear the roof! All stars!"

We were swarmed by women, and we took a bunch of pictures with our cars and motorcycles. Our sports cars and tricked-out bikes were parked out front. We were flexing, holding up money, weed, and bottles of rum. I went back inside to look for Maya, and somehow wound up at the bar. It felt like I was swept up in a wave of love from the adoring crowd who had seen what we had just done on the dance floor. It turned out that all the weeks of hard work had paid off. Practicing that routine with the bottle had nearly made me question my hand-eye coordination. But, tonight we nailed it. I toasted with Killa Bean and Casanova at the bar.

As I set my glass down, a gorgeous young lady approached the dance floor. Her walk was sultry and seductive. I had seen her around before. It was hard not to notice an ass like that. In fact, she was beautiful all the way around.

Her body was like an hourglass and her face was like a work of art. She looked like a goddess. Her crew walked in behind her. They called themselves The Laydeez.

"That's Kaydeen," said Casanova. "Ass look like a' onion!"

The Laydeez performed a sultry, sexy routine that caught the eye of every heterosexual man in the room. Grown men appeared weak in the knees at the sight of Kaydeen and her crew winding, twisting, and rolling on the floor. It was wild. Killa tapped me to follow him, and before I knew it, me and the All Star Blazers were on the floor with Kaydeen and her crew. Kaydeen grinned and came right toward me. She pushed up on me, grinding, and I gave it right back. Our dance was hot and powerful, the energy between us intense. The crowd was loving it.

Maya pushed her way through the crowd and shut it down. She pushed me off the dance floor, and I was grateful that my cousin switched the song up and kept the party going.

To my surprise, Kaydeen walked over and stepped between us.

"Well, look who it is! Maya Fenster." Kaydeen was smiling, and she looked even more gorgeous than usual. "Ya still around, eh?"

I looked from one woman to the other, confused.

"Never left yard. Unlike some of us." Maya looked at Kaydeen like she was a roach.

"Silly likkle pickney hating on mi education."

Maya balked at that. "Education? Just 'cause ya go fi school don't mean ya smart. Lek mi learn ya! Mi show ya education!"

I was worried that Maya was going to fight Kaydeen. But as she walked off toward the dance floor, I remembered where I was. This was the dancehall, where scores were settled different from the way we did things in Brooklyn.

Kaydeen looked at me, still wearing that lovely smile I was starting to enjoy too much.

"I'll be back for you, Mr. Tarzan." She winked and followed Maya to the dance floor.

I stood there, speechless. She knew my name.

Toasta threw on the track Maya had been practicing to for weeks. I knew she had been struggling with this routine. I watched as Maya and The Dutty Gals started off.

Maya was killing it. Kaydeen and her crew watched for a minute. Then they rushed the floor, and challenged them with moves of their own. The crowd roared louder for The Laydeez, and it seemed like their cheers only made Kaydeen bolder. She danced even harder, right in Maya's face. Maya gave it back. But, when Kaydeen did a headstand and popped all that booty to the beat, it was clear that The Laydeez had won. The entire dancehall went crazy, cheering, and drowning out the music.

Toasta spun the record back.

"Di winner is Tarzan! King of The Jungle!" He sounded his air horn. "He make di Dutty Gals and Di Laydeez battle for his crown! Big up!" The air horn again. I was gonna kick his ass when I got to him.

"All Star Blazers in di building!" Toasta yelled.

Kaydeen and her girls gathered together on the sidelines afterward, celebrating. I watched, sipping my cognac. I couldn't front. I was intrigued, and a little turned on by the display I had just witnessed.

Maya appeared out of nowhere and caught me staring.

"See sum'n ya want?"

"Huh?" It was all I had.

"Ya gawking over her?" Maya looked angrier than I had ever seen her before.

"What are you talking about? Nobody was gawking. You're bugging right now."

"Oh really? Buggin', eh?"

"Yeah. You're acting real insecure right now. I didn't know that's how you get down. I'm not really feeling it, to be honest with you." The look on my face said it better than my words did. The last thing I wanted was another Tameka. I had dealt with enough drama from women like that. I thought Maya was different. But, right now she was looking real familiar.

"Dat gal bad news! She nah good, Tarzan. Ya hear mi say?"

I frowned at her. "I don't understand. You said yourself that all of this shit is just dancing. That's all that was. We was all just dancing! Why are you mad? You having a fit like I was having sex with her."

"You want to?"

"Want to what?"

"Have sex with her?"

I didn't want to lie. At that point I wanted to have sex period. I had been so focused on Maya that I still hadn't crossed that hurdle since my release from jail.

"I don't even know her!"

"It don't matter. Answer mi question! Ya wan' sex her?"

"I'm gonna tell you one more time. It's just dancing. Remember that concept, Maya? You're the one who taught it to me."

"Ya wan' sex that skank? Go head!"

"Maybe I should since *you* won't give me none."

The minute I said it I realized it was a mistake. Maya looked at me, crushed, and slapped the shit out of me. By the time I recovered, she was gone.

She had caused a scene and now everyone was looking at me for all the wrong reasons. I turned to Casanova behind the bar. He had seen the whole thing.

"Mr. Casanova. Lemme get a Red Stripe. I need it. Right now."

He handed me the beer, and I took a long sip.

"It better to lose a woman," he said, "than to lose ya character. Another soon come."

I nodded. "Okay. You're the Casanova. You know women better than I do."

Casanova cleared his throat, and tapped me on the shoulder. He gestured slyly toward Kaydeen, walking toward us. The sway of her hips was mesmerizing.

"Another soon come," Casanova repeated.

SENSUAL SEDUCTION

K aydeen approached. This time, her smile wasn't as broad. It looked sympathetic.

"Are you okay? I saw that likkle scene a minute ago. She seemed upset."

"Yeah. Sorry you had to see that. But, I'm good. Thank you."

"My name is Kaydeen."

"I'm—"

"Tarzan. The Yankee." She held my gaze, her eyes full of mischief.

"I see you've done your research."

"I heard a ting or two." She was smiling wider now. Several people at the bar interrupted and asked for pictures with her. She was gracious, and allowed it. Then, she gave her attention back to me.

I commented on it.

"I guess I should be doing my research, too. Because everybody around here is treating you like royalty or something."

"I am royalty. Ya don't know?"

I laughed. She didn't. She seemed serious.

"I grew up around here," she said.

"Really?" I nodded. "Beautiful place."

"It is. I went to school abroad, though. I finished high school in the UK and currently I'm a student at Juilliard."

"In New York?"

"Yes, sir."

"I'm from Brooklyn."

"I heard." She winked.

"Oh, that's right. Your research."

She shrugged. Again, we were interrupted by her adoring crowd.

When I had her attention again, I offered her a drink. She ordered a gin and tonic. A tough drink for such a delicate thang.

"So, you said you went to school in the UK. Why don't you speak with a British accent?"

She smirked. "Jamaicans don't always speak patois, you know?" She put on a crisp British accent that would have impressed the queen. "I also got my New York swagger, too." Now, she sounded like one of Tameka's friends. "You know what I'm saying, son?"

I was impressed. "Okay, damn, Wonder Woman! You speak Chinese, too?"

She took a sip of her drink. "Well, actually, I do speak a little Mandarin."

She saw the skeptical expression on my face.

"I have a little Chinese in my blood, too."

"You're like the United Nations up in here." She did have that exotic look. Long wavy hair, light skin, and striking eyes.

"I like to think of myself as an international woman of mystery."

"Okay. Well, one mystery I need solved is what's up with you and Maya?"

She shrugged off the question and sipped her drink again. "The bishop's daughter? She's just red eye." She waved her hand, dramatically. "She's been jealous of me ever since grade school."

"Jealous? Really? Maya never seemed like the jealous type."

At least not before tonight. I had seen a very ugly side of her that evening, and it was unexpected.

"You never know a dog until you step 'pon its tail." Kaydeen looked at me, seriously.

I thought about that.

"Come hang," she said. "We can talk at my table."

I followed her to the VIP section upstairs. Killa and the crew followed suit. I had my eyes open for Dada, but I didn't see him. Kutan was there, though. So, I made sure to stay alert.

Kaydeen had a little table in the corner where a few of her girls were seated. They smiled when I approached. Kaydeen introduced us, but I was too twisted by then to remember names.

"Tarzan, this is The Laydeez crew."

"Pleasure is all mine," I said. "I saw you doing your thing out there on the floor. Nice moves. You made it hard for me and my boys to keep up."

There were bottles on the table, and I could tell Kaydeen and her crew were balling.

"I see you ladies are having a good time tonight."

"It's a lifestyle. A lady should be treated like a lady. Girls nah know 'bout this life. This is a woman ting."

"Seems like you and my lady don't get along too well."

Her friends went off to dance and Kaydeen and I sat down.

"She's yours, eh?"

"Something like that."

She made a sad face. "That's too bad." She shrugged. "The bishop's daughter and I have never been close. She doesn't really care for mi family."

"Who's your family?"

It seemed like something out of a movie. Like a dark cloud descended on us then, and I could sense that something had shifted in the atmosphere. It was the most ominous answer to my question.

"Soft cha-cha boy. What ya do over here wit mi sister?"

I heard Dada's voice, and a cold chill ran down my spine. I stood up and faced him. Two of his goons stood behind him. Kutan was nearby, watching like always.

"Oh. Okay. I see. So, this is your sister?"

Kaydeen stood up, too.

"Donovan, I'm fine. We are just sitting here talking. Go away."

Dada was smirking at me, but I could tell he didn't find this funny at all.

"Yankee! Don't put ya hat where ya can't reach it. Dis sail too fancy for ya boat, ya hear me? Ya nah belong here. Ya nah good enough to sit with mi family."

"Look, white boy, you don't even know me. Your goons and all that gully talk don't scare me. I'm sitting here." I sat back down to illustrate my point. "And until the lady wants me to leave, I will continue to sit here."

My boys stepped up. Killa Bean and the All Star Blazers rushed forward, ready for war. They stood behind me, facing Dada and his crew.

Dada sucked his teeth. "Aww. Him a badman, eh? Well, I come here to give you straight talk. The Jungle. Kingston. Jamaica. It's all mine. My property. You operate here. You operate 'pon di streets. You report to me. Ya understand?"

I looked at my boys and laughed.

"I don't report to nobody."

Dada laughed, too.

"You are a long way from home, Yankee boy. You better be careful who ya make enemies with."

This was nothing new to me. Turf wars and bullies like Dada who thought they could tell other men where they could get money—that was old news. I had dealt with that back in East New York. Dudes thought they could be selfish and keep all the wealth to themselves. It sounded like that's what this clown was accustomed to. His rich daddy had somehow managed to secure the majority of the island's wealth. Now, Dada thought that entitled him to stomp around Kingston and do the same. It was all a joke to me, and I had to resist the urge to spit in his face. That's how little I respected him and everything he stood for. Dada thought he was a kingpin, when all he would ever be was a pussy.

"I'm here," I said. "This is my home now, too. I ain't going nowhere. So, you and your friends should probably get out of my face."

I stood up to face Dada eye to eye. His goons drew their guns.

Killa Bean pulled out his machete. The look of it alone was menacing. The fact that he had used it before with deadly results was an unspoken fact.

Dada looked at Killa Bean.

"Ya better be pulling that knife out to butter mi bread!"

My boys pressed in closer, and I stepped forward, too. I was ready for whatever. I knew at that moment that I might die tonight. Dada had a point to prove, and a reputation to uphold. Everything I had been told about him indicated that he was the type to stop at nothing to prove a point. But, so was I. And, I was ready to take this shit all the way.

Kaydeen stepped in between us. Mr. Casanova noticed what was happening and summoned his guards over. They rushed in with their guns drawn.

The place was eerily silent with everyone's weapons drawn.

Dada was smiling. "Now it's a party!"

"Donovan, stop!" Kaydeen's voice cracked with emotion. She seemed to know that her brother and I were both capable of taking this all the way. "I said I was fine. As a matter of fact, we were just leaving. Right, Tarzan?" She looked at me. "Right?"

I didn't say anything. I just kept staring her brother down, unfazed. I wasn't scared of this bitch ass rich boy. He was nothing to me. I knew this guy would never survive where I came from. Here, they treated him and his family like royalty because they owned the town. But, in my eyes, he was a piece of shit. And I was starting to wonder whether his sister was trouble, too.

"Yeah, right," I said.

She led me out. I felt Dada's glare on my neck the whole time I walked. The All Star Blazers followed me out, with Killa Bean exiting last with his machete still in hand. As we got to the stairs, I heard Dada laugh loudly.

"A man almost died tonight!" he yelled. "Let's celebrate the miracle!"

I kept walking. As I descended the stairs, I locked eyes with Toasta in the deejay booth. The expression on his face told me all I needed to know. He had seen it all. And he was as livid as I was.

I walked outside with Kaydeen.

"I'm sorry about my brother," she said. "I didn't expect him to act like that."

"You don't have to apologize for Dada," I said. "He's a grown man. He does what he wants. But why didn't you tell me that you're his sister?"

"Because I didn't want you to make up your mind about me before you got to know me. That's why." She sighed. "Dada is my brother. I love him. But, he and I are not the same. I'm nothing like him."

I wasn't sure.

"It's all good. Now I see why everyone was treating you like the Queen of Jamaica. It's because you are the Queen of Jamaica. You're the daughter of a billionaire."

"What my family has or what they do is not me. That's one of the reasons I left this place. To get away from all of the things that come along with being a Davidson. When I'm in London or New York, people get to know me for who I really am. I was hoping you could, too."

"I understand that." It was true. I knew what it was like

to try and escape your former self. To be desperate to shed an old layer of your story that other people won't let you shake off.

She touched my arm, tenderly, and looked at me. "You need to be careful, Tarzan."

I frowned. "Why do you say that?"

"My brother is crazy."

I laughed. Again, she didn't.

"I'm serious. It's not a game. This is only the beginning. Trust me. He's going to try and ruin you."

I shrugged my shoulders. It wasn't that I was fearless. I had enough sense to know when I was outmatched. But, Dada was the victim of too many yes-men. People had bowed to him for so long that now he believed his own hype. I saw through all the smoke and mirrors. To me, it was clear the dude was a fraud.

"He can't ruin me."

She sucked her teeth and looked away. She shook her head in frustration, and looked at me again. "See, Tarzan? That's the attitude that's going to get you killed."

I felt an eerie shiver when she said that. I shrugged it off. I'd been drinking a lot tonight. "If that's what you think."

She didn't relent. "What if I'm not there to stop him next time?"

I turned to face her, desperate for her to understand what I was saying. I locked eyes with her and spoke slowly. "I'm not scared of your punk ass brother. I don't need nobody to step in for me. You don't know me, sweetheart."

"That's not what I meant. You don't have to be scared. To keep it real, I like the fact that you're not scared of him."

I relaxed a little.

"I'm just saying. If you test him, Donovan will try and kill you. I'm not trying to scare you. I'm just telling you what I know."

I shrugged again, and walked off toward my motorcycle. As far as I was concerned, the conversation was over. But, for some reason, Kaydeen followed me.

"Good night," I called over my shoulder. "It was nice meeting you."

I hopped on my bike.

"Just, please, be careful." Her voice was pleading.

"Good night."

I revved the engine and took off for home. I'd had enough of The Jungle for one night.

DOUBLE CROSSED

I rode my bike through the island's hills and vegetation. It would have been a gorgeous and picturesque scene if I wasn't preoccupied by the things I had on my mind. I was stressed about Maya storming out the way she had. I was still upset she had slapped me. My pride was wounded, especially because she had done it in front of so many people. But, to top it off, I was tripping out over the fact that Kaydeen—the stunning beauty who was hypnotizing and sultry—was the sister of a man I hated.

I knew Dada's type. Men who used their wealth and privilege to their advantage, stepping all over the ones beneath them. I'd seen the way he hustled Raddy Rich into being part of his crew. He was a bully, taking advantage of those less powerful than he was. No matter how high he turned up the heat, I wasn't going to let him see me sweat. I was sure that if I played my position the right way, I could take over and expose this pussy Dada as the coward I knew he was.

I pulled up at Peta Gaye and Toasta's place. I knew that Toasta was still back at The Jungle. But, I thought Maya might have gone there after the way she stormed out of the club.

I walked up to the door and knocked.

Peta Gaye answered the door in her night robe, half-awake.

"Peta Gaye, sorry to wake you." I realized I was developing a bit of a Jamaican accent after being there for so long. "Is Maya here?"

"No, Tarzan."

"Are you sure?" I peeked around her, hoping to catch a glimpse of Maya behind her.

"Yes. I'm sure. Unlike you, she's probably being thoughtful. Considerate. She probably nah wan' wake up the pickney. So she went to mi father's house to sleep."

I nodded. "Okay. I'm really sorry. When you do see her, please just have her call me immediately."

She nodded. "I'll do mi best, Tarzan." She narrowed her eyes. "So. Where's ya ras clot cousin?"

Ras clot was such a vulgar term that I winced when she said it. "Still at The Jungle," I said. I was so sorry I came here.

"The Jungle, eh? Well him a coo-coo bird so him stay there!"

I shook my head, apologized again, and started walking back toward my motorcycle.

"Tell him spend di night at home for once! Like a real husband and father! Mi sick up to here with dis dancehall fuckery!"

She slammed the door shut and I took off on my motorcycle. I pulled up at the bishop's house moments later.

I knew, as I approached the house, that I was bugging. It was late—well after midnight—and I was walking up to her father's home. This was a man who had already expressed his disapproval of me. But, tonight, I was desperate. I needed to see my baby.

I tapped softly on the window.

I called out her name in an anxious whisper. "Maya! Aye, Maya!"

I tapped on the window again, this time a little harder.

"Maya! I know you're in there. I just want to talk to you."

Suddenly, the lights in the front room came on. I could see a silhouette moving through the room toward the window. The person opened it up.

It was the bishop.

"Apparently, mi daughter nah wan' speak to you, Tarzan."

"I'm sorry, sir."

"Indeed. You are sorry. What kind of man harasses a young lady in di middle of the night?"

"Bishop, I was just—"

"Heathen! Get away! Mi rebuke you."

I was trying not to laugh. At the same time, I was aware that he was insulting me.

"I really just need to talk to her for a second, Mr. Fenster."

"She nah wan' talk! Leave now!" He pointed a trembling finger toward the road.

I stood there for a second too long.

"Demon! Go!"

That was going too far.

"Mr. Fenster—"

"Leave!"

I turned around before I got disrespectful with Maya's father. I walked toward my bike, and as I walked I could hear him yelling inside his house.

"See, Maya? Dis why mi tell you to stay away from dat dancehall! It's nah place for a bishop's daughter. Dat boy is a sinner and him a no-good Yankee man! You wan' end up like ya sister? Five kids and nah pot fi piss in?"

Clearly, he was vexed and I had only made things worse for Maya. Probably for poor Peta Gaye and Toasta, too. I decided to just go home and call it a night. As well as things had gone for the All Star Blazers, everything else had crashed and burned.

I sped off and got on the highway, steering my bike in the direction of my villa. It was a familiar route I had taken many times before. But, tonight something felt off. In fact, there had been an eerie sense of doom all night long. I couldn't put my finger on it, until I saw the flashing lights of police cars closing in behind me. This was my worst nightmare.

I glanced around and saw that they had me surrounded. I pulled over. Just when I thought things couldn't get any worse, they did just that. I had pissed Maya off, almost gotten shot, and now I was hemmed up on the side of a Kingston road with the shady Jamaican police.

This all seemed a little too coincidental. Kaydeen's warnings from earlier in the evening echoed in my ears now. Maya, too, had urged me not to cross Dada. I could almost hear the sound of his arrogant laughter in my ears now as they placed handcuffs on me without ever bothering to tell me what I was being charged with.

They put me in the back of one of their most raggedy

police cars, and drove me to jail. They booked me, and tossed me in a stone-walled hole that reeked of piss. I stood completely nude as the officer searched me for the umpteenth time. They wouldn't tell me what they were looking for. When he was done, he made me stand in the corner, still naked, while they rummaged through my clothes. This was all just an attempt to humiliate me. I held my head high, and didn't protest. The last thing I wanted was to make more enemies in this town than I already had.

They finally found a knife in the waistband of my jeans. They found some weed in my shoe and a bunch of cash in my pockets. That was it. But, that was enough. They locked me up with no judge, no jury, nothing. Just the awful sound of the metal bars clanging shut and the menacing, ceaseless pressure of my own thoughts.

By the time the sun came up, I learned that the police had ransacked my villa. They found even more cash, two more guns, and a ton of weed, and destroyed everything I had. At least that was what they told me. I had no way of knowing what was really going on. I was at the mercy of a few guards who were kind enough to feed me updates like a dog waiting beneath the dinner table for falling crumbs. I snatched up each nugget of information hungrily. I was anxious about how my family and friends were doing in the midst of Dada's ruthless quest for vengeance.

I was aware that I had fucked up. I was locked up in a foreign country with some powerful adversaries. I wouldn't admit to myself that I was scared. But, I knew that the situation I was facing was serious.

Everything they found could keep me in prison here for a very long time. For as long as they liked, really. The government here was corrupt. Surely, there were officials in Dada's pocket. People who could see to it that I was locked away for years. Already I could tell that this system was completely different from the one I had sadly become accustomed to in America. I didn't get a lawyer. No phone call. Nothing. This was not the due process I was used to. Here, the police didn't play. I was thrown in a cell to rot. Kaydeen had warned me that this was only the beginning. Now, I knew that she'd meant what she said. Dada had it out for me and my whole squad.

Days passed, and I learned from the officers assigned to guard me that they had raided Toasta's house. The news hit me hard. I thought about my cousin, about Peta Gaye and the children, and I felt terrible. I had come into their lives and brought so much destruction and chaos. One of the guards told me that the police had torched Toasta's brand-new BMW. I knew that alone had broken my cousin's heart. He loved that car so much. To him, it was more than just a vehicle. That car represented all the hard work he'd put in for years in pursuit of his goals. Upgrading from the trash box he'd picked me up in at the Kingston airport to the shiny new ride he'd purchased recently was a huge accomplishment in Toasta's life. Having it destroyed was just another cruel joke, courtesy of Dada's twisted, evil mind.

That wasn't all. The same guard told me about what happened to my friend. Killa had caught the worst of Dada's wrath.

I knew when Killa pulled out his machete in The Jungle that Dada would never let that slide. Something in the way he had looked at Killa Bean made it clear that this was not the end. I was right. The guard informed me that Dada's goons had caught Killa Bean slipping. After a night at The Jungle, Killa had been heading to his car. Kutan was there, and he ordered his men to pin Killa down in the middle of the street. While Killa fought with all his might, Kutan had taken his machete and carved the word "Dada" into Killa's chest, branding him for life. Then he sliced my boy across his face for good measure, scarring him even further. The word on the street was that Killa Bean's blood had stained the streets of Kingston for days afterward. I was physically sick when I got the news. I felt powerless.

I was devastated. Then I found out that Farmer was locked up, too. The police rode up to the mountainside, and found him in his lair, surrounded by marijuana plants. They led him to the car, still smoking his blunt. The police who escorted him even respected Farmer. He was the man. A legend in these parts. Dada was playing dirty. Farmer had been in business for a long time. He wasn't bothering anyone. For decades, he had existed on the mountainside of Jamaica, growing his ganja and selling to local hustlers. The problem was that he had been supplying me. He had dared to distribute to the one man Dada wanted gone by any means. I had a bull's-eye on my back, and everyone around me was going down in flames.

Then came the day when I learned that Uncle Screechie's restaurant had been raided. The police had come in using unnecessary force, busted up the place, scared off all the patrons, and punched Uncle Screechie in the gut for good measure. They found no guns or drugs, but helped themselves to carloads of food they stole just to rub salt in our wounds.

I wasn't having a picnic, either. Every day, the guards pulled me out of my cell and beat me. Sometimes until I was unconscious. When I wasn't getting my ass beat by the cops, the other prisoners ganged up on me. There was no law and order in here. I was in a place where the inmates ran the jail and the guards looked the other way. My days were spent fighting for my life, and wishing I could get a do-over for some of the things I'd said and done.

This was all too familiar. I had promised myself that I would never be in this type of situation again. My life was beginning to feel like it was going in cycles. Sometimes up. Most times down. I was in a repetitive spiral of negative bullshit. Again, I was forced to face the enemy within me. My pride. It drove me to do things I regretted later. I'd allowed my pride to run me out of Brooklyn. Now, here I was in Kingston, locked up again. I was sick of myself. Alone in my cell, for the first time in years, I cried.

I could hear my mama's voice in my ears. She always told me that if you hit the bottom, you're in the perfect position for prayer. So, I closed my eyes, got on my knees on the filthy stone floor of my jail cell, and prayed.

Lord, if You're real, show me. Show up for me now. I need You. I never tried this before. Praying ain't something I do. So, I'm asking You to forgive me for my sins. Mama said that You know my heart. So You know that I'm a good man. I have good intentions at least. I just want to take care of my family. I just want to provide for everyone that I love. And sometimes I go about it the wrong way. Please change the way that I think. Help me fix the way that I react to certain situations. Change me. Have mercy on me, God. Amen.

I prayed off and on several times that night. I cried a little more, too. Before I knew it, the sun was up and it was time to face another day.

I woke up early. It was something I had learned to do as a defense mechanism. The earlier I woke up, the sooner I could face whatever the guards and inmates were going to hit me with today.

I did some push-ups in my cell, and got myself ready for war. I heard a guard approach and wondered which one of them it was today. Some of them pretended to be cool. Others were straight assholes. Either way, I was ready.

"Yankee man! Ya made bail!"

I was shocked. "I did?"

The guard opened my cell and I stepped out. He led me down the cell block toward an office down the hall. They processed my paperwork with grunts and mumbles, and then escorted me out of the building. I walked out, squinting from the sun.

Maya and Bishop were waiting for me. It took all of my restraint to walk and not run in Maya's direction. I had never been so happy to see anyone in my whole life. I thought about my prayers last night. As I walked toward Maya and her father, I glanced quickly skyward, and said, "Thank you."

GOOD AND EVIL

Bishop was giving me a very cold stare. I pretended not to notice. I was so relieved to be free. Or at least I was free for now. One of the police was still alongside me. Together, we walked over to where Maya and her father stood, and greeted them.

"Here you go, Bishop. He's all yours," the officer said.

"Thank you, my good man. See you in service on Sunday, eh?"

The officer nodded. "Ya know mi never miss a day. God bless you, Bishop."

I was surprised. I shook the bishop's hand as the officer walked away.

"Thank you, sir." I was truly appreciative. "You literally answered my prayers. I mean that."

He gave me a cold and icy stare. "No. Maya answered them."

She looked at me, shyly. "I knew that my father could help. He worked at the embassy for all those years and made a lot of friends."

Bishop was still eyeing me. "Save the lost. Dis is my calling. Maya has been hounding me for days to get involved and help you."

"Well, I appreciate it, Bishop."

I wondered why we were still standing there. I wanted to get away from this hellish place.

"Ya still not off free," he said. "There will be a fair trial. An investigation. All of that soon come."

"I'm just glad to be out of there."

I hugged Maya, careful to keep my hands in respectful places in the presence of her father.

"And I'm happy to see you," I said to her.

She looked at me, her eyes full of affection. "You, too."

I lost myself for a moment and leaned forward to kiss her. But, Bishop put his hand in my face, preventing me from going in.

"You want to go back in that jail? Because I will be happy to join you."

I let Maya go, and the three of us headed to the car, finally. I climbed in the back, and Maya sat up front with her father. He had the radio on at a low volume. I was nervous. The last time I had encountered this guy, he wasn't very pleasant. I hoped to keep the conversation to a minimum. But, the bishop kept grilling me in the rearview mirror. He was staring at me so hard that it felt like he expected me to say something. I cleared my throat.

"You don't know how much I appreciate you bailing me out. Jamaican prison is no joke. Thank you, Bishop."

The bishop grunted. "Hopefully I nah waste my time."

I thought about the way I had cried and prayed myself to sleep last night. Now, here I was riding free with my girl. I had to believe that God had a hand in it.

"I was starting to lose hope in there," I said. "Each night I slept with one eye open. And each morning I woke up ready to fight. But, last night I prayed. It was the first time I did it in a very long time. My mama used to try to convince me that it works. But, I never saw the proof. Until today. Last night, I talked to God and poured my heart out. Now, here I am riding in the car with you two." I shook my head, amazed. "This praying stuff might actually work."

Bishop chuckled. "Yes, young man. Maybe the Bible is more than your little tattoos that you have inked all over your body. Which, by the way, is blasphemous."

I looked down at all my tattoos peeking out from beneath my tank top. I tried to cover them with my tattered jacket.

"I don't know about all of that," I said, honestly. "Like I told you before, I don't really read the Bible and all that. I just try to live my life right. And now I'm trying to get myself on the right path."

Bishop glanced at me in the mirror again. "The path has always been there for man to walk. It's just too narrow for cowards and for the weak. The steps of a good man are ordered by the Lord, Tarzan. Being righteous is a choice. Choose *life*, young man. Not death."

Maya touched his arm, gently. "Papa, it's Sunday. We already heard your sermon for the day." She smiled, and it seemed to melt his heart just like it did mine.

"Maya, you must not run from righteousness. That's how you get mixed up with the wrong people. Then you beg me for help. Well, that's what I'm trying to do here. Help your friend."

I wondered if he forgot that I was sitting right there and

I could hear every word he said. He was talking about me
like I was invisible.

"He has been lost," he continued. "And my words are
like bread crumbs. He's being fed and led with spiritual
food. He's hungry, Maya! Starving for inspiration."

I sat in silence for a while. Finally, I laughed.

"After being in that cell for so long, I'm so hungry and
starving right now for any kind of food. Are we going somewhere to eat?"

Maya laughed. Her father did not. Bishop shook his head,
while she turned up the radio. A commercial was on about
the upcoming dance clash at The Jungle.

> *For the first time ever, Kingston Rhythm pres-
> ents the ten-million-dollar dancehall clash! Who
> will be crowned King of the Dancehall? It's the
> ultimate dancehall clash. Dancers from all over
> the island. Be there! Next Saturday night at The
> Jungle. Registration begins at 9:00 P.M. This is
> the ten-million-dollar dancehall clash! Don't
> miss it!*

My ears perked up at the sound of that. The truth was,
I needed money fast. Farmer was still locked up. So, there
was no possibility of getting back on my feet the easy way.
For once, I thought I might try to win something the good
old-fashioned way. Through all the hard work that Killa
and I had been putting in with the All Star Blazers. I
glanced at Bishop in the front seat and thought about what
he'd just been saying. I was willing to try to go legit. Maybe
there was something to this dancehall thing after all.

Bishop drove me to my place. The closer we got, my adrenaline pumped so high that I thought they could hear my heartbeat in the car. The moment we rounded the corner, though, it was clear that there wasn't much left to salvage. All of the windows had been knocked out. Glass and debris were everywhere. The front door had been left wide open. I walked inside, stepping on broken glass, and found my clothes burned and much of my stuff missing. I stood for a moment in the silence and let the truth sink in. Everything I had was gone.

I was angry. But, I pushed my emotions down deep and faced Bishop, standing in the doorway.

"Okay," I said. "I've seen it for myself. We can go now." I was fighting back tears of rage. The last thing I wanted to do was let one fall in front of Bishop. Or in front of Maya, who was standing behind him. "You can bring me to my cousin's house, if you don't mind."

Bishop stood looking at me, strangely. Finally, he looked me in the eye and spoke.

"This was the same scene at your uncle's restaurant. And it would have been the case at mi daughter's home. But, thankfully, I was there to intervene." He shook his head. "You've brought a lot of pain to a lot of people, Tarzan."

I stared at the man. It felt like he was rubbing salt in my wounds when I was already knocked out.

Maya stepped forward. "Daddy." It was all she said. But, it did its job and broke the tension.

Bishop looked at her. He turned and headed back toward his car. "Okay. Tarzan, let's go. I will bring you to your cousin's house now."

I looked around one more time, and then followed him and Maya out. Once we got back in the car, I thought about what Bishop might be trying to tell me. It was true. I had brought a lot of pain to a lot of people. But, my intentions had been good. The past few weeks had shown me how dangerously I was living. It was like I had been existing on the side of a cliff and was somehow surprised when I fell over the edge. We rode in silence for a while before any of us said a word. It was me who broke the silence. My mind was racing, desperate for ways to make things right without ever going back to prison again.

"If I won that dance clash, I could get enough money for me to get my life straight." I thought about it as I stared out the window. "I would have to split it with the All Star Blazers. But, still, that would be enough to get me on my feet. Help me walk the straight and narrow."

I looked at the bishop. He was staring at me in the rearview mirror, hanging on my every word.

"Maybe it's time for me to make a righteous step."

Bishop smirked. "People willing to reward youths for winding and grinding 'pon each other? Mi nah understand this mind-set."

"That's because you're old, Daddy." Maya gave him a wink.

"The older the moon, the brighter it shines." Bishop was smiling. "I just can't imagine what the fascination is with this dancehall foolery. I wish I could get you away from that world."

He eyed me when he said that last part.

I cleared my throat and tried to reason with Bishop. "It's just like what you teach in church. It's spiritual. It's a connection to our soul. It allows people to relate to one another."

"Yeah," Maya agreed. "The dancehall is our church."

He looked at her seriously. "Don't say that. God is not pleased with that."

I was sick of the bishop and his judgmental attitude.

"No disrespect," I said. "But, it's our common meeting ground. It's the place where we fellowship. The dancehall is the place where we can be ourselves and get closer to God. Except in our 'church,' the people aren't judgmental hypocrites."

The bishop sucked his teeth so hard, I wished I could take my words back.

"Daddy—" Maya tried to intervene.

"No, Maya! I've tried to be nice to your little friend. But, I will not stand for the disrespect." He turned his sights on me again. "Ya nah get close to God grinding and winding your bodies. You are ridiculous. Clearly, your ignorant, thuggish ways have gotten you nowhere in life. I knew it was a poor idea to get a hoodlum out of jail!"

"Daddy!" Maya was crying now.

"The boy is lost, Maya. I don't want you around him."

"You don't understand."

"Of course I do. I was young once. I understand exactly what he is. And what he wants from you. I try my hardest to protect you. But, it's like you are drawn to wickedness."

"No, I am not."

"All this dancehall madness. Dreadlocks, ganja, and tattooed hoodlums. You are headed down a path of destruction. You want to end up like your sister here? Living in a shack with no money and five kids? I don't want that for your life."

"With all due respect, please don't speak about my family like that." I was trying so hard not to go off on this man.

He stopped the car about half a mile short of Toasta and Peta Gaye's house. I sat there for a moment before it dawned on me that he meant for me to get out. Maya was pleading my case. But, the bishop wasn't trying to hear it. Finally, I opened the door to get out.

"Look, sir. I'm sorry if I offended you. Those were not my intentions."

"I feel your intentions are always sorry. You need to change. You are causing a lot of trouble around here and bringing a lot of people grief. Your uncle Screechie, for instance, is a good man who doesn't deserve the trouble. The Lord put it on my heart to come help you because I believe they would have really killed you in that jail. Honestly, mi nah think it's a good idea for you to be around my family. Or even in Jamaica, for that matter. My advice is to go back to where you came from."

I nodded. "No matter where I go, I'm always going to be me. I wish you could see the true me because I am not the person you think I am."

"Words are a lot easier than actions."

"Well, watch this action."

I got out of the car and slammed the door. I began walking the long road to Toasta's house.

NEW DIRECTION

I tried to shake off my anger the whole time I walked to my cousin's house. I was furious that Maya's father thought it was okay to talk down to me like that. I had made my share of mistakes. But, I wasn't the worthless piece of trash he was making me out to be.

When I got to Toasta's house, he was hanging out in the front yard with his kids. As I approached, I noticed the charred remains of his BMW still parked in the same spot where Dada's people had set it on fire. Instantly, I felt a wave of guilt wash over me. I knew how much my beef with Dada had cost the people close to me. The weight of that was killing me. Bishop's words echoed in my mind, adding insult to injury.

To my surprise, Toasta was in high spirits. He was dancing and laughing with his kids as I approached. When he spotted me, he rushed over and hugged me. He stepped back and looked me over, making sure I was in one piece.

"Brethren! Ya all right?"

"Aye," I said. "I'm still standing. The bishop just tried to mess up my day. But, I ain't letting him get to me." I waved it off, telling myself to let it go. "Anyway, damn." I gestured toward his car. "I see they got the new Beamer."

He sighed. "Yeah. But, dem small tings to a giant! I'm good. You're good. The family is good. That's all that matters."

I shrugged. "Yeah, but now, everything is fucked up."

"Nah. Mi mixtapes is selling like crazy. I'm telling you, I'm gonna have a hit soon. Trust me. We can't be stopped out here. All Star Blazers for life!"

I nodded. "That's what I'm talking about."

I liked his optimistic attitude. I needed that right now. My thoughts drifted quickly, though.

"How is Killa Bean?"

"He's a'ight. Got a buck fifty across his face. But, he sees it as his stripes and battle wounds. Tribal scars. He'll be fine. Him a badman."

"I hate that everybody's caught up in my shit." Saying it out loud, I felt the weight on my shoulders lift a little.

"We squad. Your shit is our shit, fam! Just like I said. All Star Blazers for life!"

I nodded. "Word. All Star Blazers for life!"

Toasta lowered his voice. "I just got word that they let Farmer out, too."

My eyes went wide. "Yeah?"

"Yes. So, we can jump back in where we left off."

I thought about it. The thought was tempting. Nothing would satisfy me more than getting back on my feet and showing Dada that he couldn't stop me. But, the knowledge that I had caused my family and friends so much pain and trouble was haunting me. I knew it was time for a change.

"Nah," I said. "I think I'm done with that life, bro."

Toasta stared at me like I was an imposter.

"Come again? I don't know if I heard ya right."

"Man, I'm for real. I'm not trying to see the inside of another jail cell. Not in the States. Not in Jamaica. Not on the moon."

Toasta stared at me for just a moment longer before he slowly nodded. "I feel dat. It's just the money was so easy."

It was. Selling weed in Jamaica—good weed—was a very lucrative business. Plus, I had been getting money from my boy Kareem's frequent trips to Jamaica using the farmer's connections at the port. But, all of that was over now.

"I think there's even easier money to get."

Toasta looked at me. "Oh, yeah? How? I'm all ears."

"The ten-million-dollar dancehall clash."

Toasta looked at me, skeptically. "You do realize that's ten million Jamaican dollars, right?"

I smiled. "Yeah, nigga. I get it. But, it's still almost eighty thousand dollars in the U.S. That could get us together real quick. It can help my mom, my brother, our crew. Even help get your music right to take your career to the next level."

He thought about it and nodded. "Very true, General. That money is as good as ours. I'm riding with you all di way, brethren!"

I was relieved to hear that. "Tomorrow night, round up the squad and we'll link up at The Jungle to start practicing for the dance clash. We 'bout to get this money!"

We solidified it with a handshake hug that only brothers understand.

"Tarzan."

I turned to find Maya standing behind me. She looked embarrassed. I assumed it was because of the way her pops had just acted. She cleared her throat before she spoke.

"Can we go somewhere and talk?"

I glanced at Toasta. He smiled.

"Ya know your motorcycle was spared in all the melee."

I'd been wondering about it for the longest time, but thought it would be too selfish of me to ask considering the circumstances.

"The cops tore this place apart, looking for any ting. Lucky for you, Bishop managed to save your bike. It's parked in the back."

I was relieved. There was some bright spot in this day after all. I looked at Maya.

"You want to go for a ride?"

She nodded.

I looked around for her father, afraid that he was lurking somewhere waiting to attack me with his words again.

Maya sensed my fear. "He's gone. After you left, we sat there and argued. Daddy refused to budge. So, I got out of the car and walked here a few minutes after you did."

I smiled. *That's my girl.*

"Let's go."

We rode through the countryside together, and it felt like time stood still. Maya's body was pressed against my back, her hands clutching me tightly. I felt like the luckiest man in the world, alone with the woman I loved. Even though so much in my life was going wrong, this time alone with her felt so right.

We watched the sunset as we rode together. Then rain

began to fall, and we had to find shelter. We rode out to my place. Although it had been ransacked, we ran inside, anxious to get out of the pouring rain. As it beat down on the roof, we stood in the doorway looking around, hopelessly, at the incredible mess. Maya smiled at me.

"Time to clean up." She grabbed a broom from beneath a bunch of junk piled up on the kitchen floor, and began sweeping. She began to clear a path from the doorway through the living room.

I never felt more in love with her than I did at that moment. As hopeless as my whole life was, she was right there willing to stand by my side and help me clean up the mess. I walked over to her, kissed her, and then helped her clean up. We did our best to salvage a few things, and then we stood near what used to be the front window, watching the rain beat down on the house and the earth outside. Maya found some weed that the cops hadn't discovered during their search. She rolled it and we smoked it together.

I looked at her sitting on a cushion on the floor while she puffed the ganja. Her hair hung around her shoulders, framing her face like the mane of a lioness. I had never seen her look sexier.

"Even though your father obviously hates me, I just want to thank you for coming to get me out of jail. I don't know if I'll ever be able to explain to you what that means to me. It was hell in there." I took a long toke.

"You're welcome, baby." Her voice sounded so sweet.

"I've never had anyone really care for me like that before. Nobody besides my mama, you know what I mean? I spent five years in prison back in the U.S., and no one ever thought to even come and visit me. Let alone try to help me get out. Kinda makes a person feel worthless."

I looked out the window at the rain. The weather was gloomy, and cloudy. Exactly how I felt at the moment.

"Maybe your father is right. Maybe I need to get out of here and not be a burden on you and everyone else around me."

She sucked her teeth and put out the spliff.

"You are not a burden, Tarzan. You cannot listen to mi father. You are a blessing. You are going to win the dance clash, just like you said. And, when you do, you're going to be a blessing to so many people. Your family. My family. The All Star Blazers will win. I can feel it."

I smiled.

"Why are you so good to me?" I had to know. Maya was pure, innocent. Maybe even a little naïve. She loved me enough to defy her religious father for the sake of being by my side, encouraging me to keep going.

"Because I love you."

I felt breathless, speechless, and completely caught off guard. Finally, I found my voice.

"Those are big words. You might not want to say that to me. 'I love you' comes with a lot. A lot of passion. A lot of weight. A lot of pain."

"Mi know what it comes with."

"I don't want you to say that to me because you think that's what I need to hear right now."

She shook her head.

"That's not it. Not at all, Tarzan. I wouldn't say it if the words were empty."

"Love comes with a certain level of commitment, loyalty,

and trust. I've never been able to trust anyone in my life. Not completely. You feel me?" I looked at her, seriously. "I trust you. I love you, too, Maya."

She took my hand. "Tarzan, I think I'm ready."

I stared at her, my body reacting instantly to her words. I cleared my throat.

"Really?"

She nodded, a smile tickling the corners of her lips. "Be my king."

Those words were music to my ears. It was what I had been auditioning for the moment I set foot on a dance floor. A year ago, I never would have imagined myself vying for King of the Dancehall. But, as she leaned closer to me and kissed me deeply, I realized that I had really been striving to be king of Maya's heart.

My hands explored her body, slowly—so slowly, and tenderly. She was hungry for me, and I could feel it in her kiss. I led her to my bed, grateful even for this ransacked villa in the middle of a rainstorm because it gave us somewhere to be alone together. I peeled her out of her clothes and discarded my own. Tenderly, carefully, and with all the love I had inside, I made love to Maya, aware that she was a virgin and fragile. I felt like one, too. I hadn't been with a woman since I came home from jail. Being inside of her tight, sweet walls, it was worth the wait. I tasted every inch of her chocolate body, passionately, until she fell asleep in my arms. Our bodies glistened together in the moonlight. I lay back smoking ganja, with Maya draped across my body, and the crickets singing a chorus outside. It was the happiest moment of my life.

THE BISHOP

aya and I couldn't get enough of each other in the weeks after that. We rehearsed with our respective crews, and handled our responsibilities to our families. But, then we would steal away every chance we got and make love until she begged for mercy. I couldn't keep my hands off of her. I knew that our physical chemistry was heightened by the incredible love we shared.

I sold the last of the weed I had and sent some money home to Mama and Trent. I got my place fixed up and Maya and I made it *ours*. She filled that villa with music, laughter, and some of the best cooking I had ever had. She was loving me better than any woman ever had, and I felt blessed to call her my own.

One night, she showered, slipped into her sexy nightwear, and stood sipping a cup of ginger tea by the open window. The room was dark, and she was cloaked in the moonlight. Her dreads were pinned up in a glorious crown.

"I want to have babies with you."

She said it out of nowhere. I was caught off guard, staring at her with my mouth wide open in surprise. I stammered, struggling for a response.

"Wh—you . . . yeah?"

She nodded, giggling a little at my obvious shock. "The way I feel for you, Tarzan . . . I want to feel it always." She had a faraway look in her eyes that melted my heart. "I envision you running around being silly with our children. Loving our daughters. Nurturing our sons. I want that." She glanced at me. "Do you?"

I nodded. I wanted that more than anything. "Yeah. I do." I stared off in space, lost in thought. Each time I imagined the picture Maya had so beautifully painted, I was reminded of how I couldn't make it possible. I had no money. No hustle anymore. No way to provide for the woman I loved, the future she desired or the happy ending that we both deserved.

She watched me from where she stood.

"What's on ya mind, Tarzan? And don't tell me it's nuttin'. I can see ya wheels turning."

I sighed. "My money is gone, Maya. I'm tapped out. Usually, this is when I would do something drastic. That's what I'm used to." I looked at her, trying to gauge her reaction. "But, I'm in love with you. And that changes everything."

She exhaled, and it occurred to me that she had been holding her breath. So much was riding on me doing the right thing. Bishop had already made up his mind that I was trouble. If I went back to the life I knew, I would be proving him right and jeopardizing everything that Maya and I had managed to build together.

"Your father gives me a hard time. You know what I'm saying? He takes every opportunity to put me down, and let me know that he doesn't think I'm the best man for you. I don't always like the way he goes about it. But, I gotta respect the man for taking care of his family. He loves his daughters. And he's doing everything he can to make sure you're protected. I don't remember much about my pops. But, I know that he left. When he did, my mama had a tough time holding all the pieces together. I imagine that must be what it's like for the bishop to see Peta Gaye struggling with the kids. He doesn't want the same for you, Maya. And, neither do I. I want the same things you want. I probably want them even more than you do. But, I gotta get my shit together in order to make that happen."

She came and cuddled up with me on the bed, her head against my chest. I wrapped my arms around her and pulled her even closer.

"I don't want to spend another second away from you. If that means I gotta scrub tables at Uncle Screechie's until I become king of the dancehall, then so be it. I'm in this to win it, Maya. For real."

She kissed me, and straddled me, her hands all over my face and chest. With her touch, she told me that everything I had said was music to her ears. She whispered in my ear that she loved me.

"I *want* you." Her voice was desperate, anxious. I was turned on by her aggression, and pulled the straps down on her nightgown. I took her breasts in my hand, squeezing and tugging, tempting her to get even wilder. It worked. She sucked my lip, moaning softly, and slid her wetness down around my eager dick.

I slid into her slowly, her tight walls so tender after days of lovemaking. She slid herself around me, wrapping me in her warmth. Although she was new to this, Maya took to lovemaking like a natural. All of the moves she had mastered on the dance floor gave her plenty to work with as she rode me. She winded her hips, twirling her sex all over me, pulsating against me as she came.

I joined her soon afterward, squeezing her ass in the palms of my hands, biting my lip to keep from screaming like a girl. Maya had me ready to question all logic. It was becoming increasingly obvious that the smart thing for me to do would be to leave Kingston. To take the next flight out in the middle of the night and slip away quietly. Away from the police harassing me and my loved ones and the constant threat of Dada making my life a living hell. But, there was no way I could leave Maya behind, no way I was walking away from what we had. Maya was tied to Jamaica. Her family was here, her roots. She had no desire to leave. Definitely not for an uncertain future in America with a man her father hadn't exactly embraced. If I wanted to be with her, I had to figure out a way to stay here.

That night, Maya slept peacefully in the silent darkness of my bedroom. I watched her sleep, thinking about my next move. I was envisioning a future with her. One filled with love, laughter, and stability. I wanted to make her happy, and provide for her, protect her. I stroked her face, trying to memorize each freckle, each crease. She was so beautiful. I was a very lucky man. I barely slept that night. My thoughts were preoccupied with my concerns about Mama. I didn't want her to have to struggle to make ends meet. I wanted Trent to stay in school and not have to worry about breaking his back to provide. I needed to win the dancehall clash battle. Everything was riding on that.

I went back to work at Uncle Screechie's the next day. There wasn't much work to do, really. The restaurant was basically empty. All the tourists and most of the usual patrons had been scared away in the violent and unnecessary raid that Dada had orchestrated. Uncle Screechie had gotten word that there were specific orders to boycott the restaurant because it belonged to my family. Uncle Screechie kept a cool head, though. I tried to do the same while I watched his business suffer. I wiped down the tables, and stacked some chairs in the corner.

"General!"

The tone of alarm in Uncle Screechie's voice made me snap out of the daydream I'd been in. I looked at him and understood that he had seen me working with a dazed look on my face, and he meant to break me out.

"Pep up, ya hear me? Trouble nah set like rain, eh?" Uncle Screechie wore a grin as he addressed me.

I nodded. I prayed that he was right, and that trouble was as fleeting as rain. "Yeah, man. Uncle Screechie, I'm sorry that you got caught up in all of my bullshit."

Screechie waved his hand, not hearing that. "We family. Customers soon come. Dis nah di first time mi romp wit' Babylon. Nah worry, nephew. We stick together. Build yourself. What nah poison, only fatten."

I nodded. "Got it." I thought I did, anyway. Uncle Screechie loved a proverb, and I wasn't sure all of them made sense.

I stacked the last few chairs and took a walk out toward the shore. My cell phone rang, and I recognized the Brooklyn number immediately. I answered.

"Hey, Trent. What's good?"

"Hey, Tarzan. You okay?"

"Yeah," I lied.

"Okay." Trent sounded strange. "Listen. Mama is back in the hospital."

"What?" I closed my eyes in disbelief.

"She went to her dialysis appointment the other day. There were some complications, and she was rushed to the emergency room. She's gonna be okay. But, she'll have to stay in the hospital for a while. So, you know that means the bills are going to be crazy."

I did know. We had been down this road a thousand times before. It felt like every time we climbed out from under the mountain of Mama's medical bills, she had another setback that landed her in the hospital again. Then the process started all over like a sad song on repeat.

"Damn," I said. "Did you get the money I sent last month?"

"Yeah. That paid everything up to this point." Trent sighed. "You know I don't like to call you with this stuff. You've already done enough. And only God knows how you're making it happen."

I didn't want to get into that at all. "Listen, little bro. Don't worry. I got you. I always do. I always figure it out."

He was silent for a second, then I thought I heard him breathe a sigh of relief. He chuckled a little.

"That's why Mama named you Tarzan. Always strong."

I laughed.

"How you holding up there?" he asked. "We heard you ran into a little trouble down there on the island."

"Yeah," I said. "It's nothing. I'm all good now. Just trying to live right."

"Okay. Be careful out there, Tarzan."

"I will," I promised. "Tell Mama I love her, and give her a kiss for me. Tell her to rest up and don't worry. I'll take care of everything."

"Cool," Trent said. "Respect."

"Bless up."

I hung up and stared out into the ocean, deep in thought. I wasn't going back to jail. But, I had to do something drastic. And soon. Too many people were counting on me.

I saw Toasta as I was walking back toward the restaurant. He took one look at the expression on my face and knew I was stressed.

"What's wrong, brethren? Why ya face sad so?"

I tried to perk up. Uncle Screechie, too, had noticed my downcast eyes and the long stretches of time I spent in silent contemplation. I had so much on my mind. More than I could tell Toasta at once. But, I did my best to open up about what was worrying me most at the moment.

"My little brother called me. Mama's back in the hospital. Bills are piling up again. Looks like I might have to do something crazy to get my hands on some money, quick." I was anguished over that. "I don't want to go back to that life, Toast. I got in enough trouble doing things the hard way. I need to start moving differently. I prayed about it . . ." I stopped talking, aware that I might be saying too much. I loved my cousin. Don't get me wrong. But, revealing the details of my deepest, most private moments was going too far. I wasn't comfortable being that vulnerable yet.

"I just want to try to stay out of trouble. That's all I'm saying. I want to get my mother's bills paid, set my brother up nice, and live my life, Toast. That's it. For once I'm trying to do that shit without cracking somebody over the head for their wallet or flooding the hood with drugs."

Toasta sighed. "You know mi understand that better than anybody. I came to live with you, Trent, and Aunt Loretta in Brooklyn and everybody expected me to be a badman. They heard I was from Kingston, and they expected me to live up to all the hype. You remember."

I did. Toasta had gained a reputation and earned the respect of some of the most thorough niggas in the hood. He used his intimidating size, his Jamaican accent, and his menacing glare to his advantage. For a while, he was someone to be feared if you found yourself alone with him in a dark alley at the wrong time.

"I got used to that life. Then I came back home, and fell in love. That changed it all, Tarzan. When I laid eyes on Peta Gaye, I knew she was the woman I would marry. She had my children, and I feel honored every single day for that privilege."

My eyes widened. I knew that Toasta loved his wife. But, I had never heard him talk like this.

"I couldn't risk losing my life out there trying to prove how bad I was. Then what? I die and some natty dread come scoop up Peta Gaye and mi pickney?" He shuddered at the thought. "A man needs to stand strong for his family. No more life on the run for me."

I thought about how long I'd been running. All my life,

it seemed. Since I was young, I had been fleeing some-thing. Fleeing the local gangs looking for an easy mark back in Brooklyn. Fleeing the worst thugs in the New York State prison system while I was incarcerated there. The cops and Dada's goons here in Kingston. I wondered when I would grow weary.

"So I started doing what I love—music," Toasta said. "If that don't make me some money, I don't know what I'll do next. But, I have made up my mind to stand up to all my doubters. The bishop, Dada and his crew, everyone who doesn't see my vision. I know it will work out for us." He nodded. "I feel you, Tarzan. It's hard out here for us. But, if you think Kingston is where you belong, if Maya is the woman you want a future with, you have to find a way to figure it out. I'm gonna do all I can to help ya out, brethren. Trust."

I nodded. He gave me a hug/handshake and gestured toward his beat-up Beamer.

"I'm heading home. Promised Peta Gaye no dancehall tonight." He rolled his eyes.

I laughed. "One night won't hurt you. Casanova will figure it out."

Toasta left, and I finished up at Uncle Screechie's and jumped on my bike. I went directly to the church, where I found the bishop in the sanctuary alone. I stepped inside and felt the peace and silence wrap around me like a warm blanket. I had often expressed my doubts about religion. But, there was no question that there was a presence in that cathedral that was out of this world.

The bishop turned and faced me when I approached.

"Listen. I don't want to waste your time," I said. "I just

came to thank you for using your connections to get me out of jail. You didn't have to do it. But, for your daughter . . . or for whatever reason, you did it. And, I'm grateful." I cleared my throat. "And I want to apologize for the things I said to you last time. We might not agree on everything. But, that doesn't give me a right to be disrespectful." I glanced around, feeling slightly awkward. I looked at the bishop again. "I may not have all the answers. I'm starting to realize that."

He stared at me for a while. I waited for the verbal assault I was used to receiving from him by now. Instead, he sat down on the nearest pew, and motioned for me to take a seat as well. I sat on a bench near him. I was close, but still far enough for me to get away if he tried to do an exorcism or something.

He began speaking, his voice as authoritative as usual.

"When mi wife died, I was heartbroken. Not only had I lost the woman who made my earth spin. But, I was alone to raise two daughters by mi self. It was no walk in di park. I wanted them to know that they are queens. Not hoochie mamas. Queens!"

His voice reverberated in the sanctuary, and I nodded so that he would calm down.

"I told them to reserve themselves for kings. Men worthy of the crown jewels, if ya know what I mean."

I did.

"Along came your family. Your cousin Allester came along and stole Peta Gaye's heart. Her life has been tough since then. A struggle. Allester has not always done tings the way that I would have suggested. But, that is her husband. I can do nothing but pray for her."

He shook his head, wringing his hands, helplessly.

"Maya is mi baby gal. She is an innocent flower. At least to me she is. She has a beauty that resonates from within. And the body of her mother. The kind of curves that make men turn dey heads. You are not di first badman to set his sights on mi daughter. I am a lion when it comes to them for a reason. I will not sit idly by and watch Maya throw away her promising future because of the foolishness of youth." He stopped speaking for a moment, and seemed to gather his thoughts. He cleared his throat. "So, I have been very hard on you, Tarzan. *Very* hard. Because I know that Maya is special. She is truly worthy of a man who will lead her down di correct path." He looked at me. "I am still not certain that you are such a man." He shrugged. "Still, Maya has assured me that she loves you. She says that you love her as well."

"I do, Bishop. I love Maya very much." I meant it. I had never felt this way before.

He nodded. "Then do di right thing, Tarzan. I still do not tink you are safe here in Jamaica. It seems there are badmen after you. I don' wan' mi daughter gettin' caught up in none of that."

"I will give my life to protect, Maya, Bishop. I promise you that. But I'm not leaving Jamaica. This is Maya's home. And, it's my home now, too."

He stood up. "Maya is a woman now. She can make her own decisions. I will not stand in di way. But, I want you to know that I got mi eyes on you. If ya hurt mi daughter, Tarzan Brixton, I will never forgive you."

He walked out, leaving me alone in the silence. I sat there for a few minutes, thinking about everything. When

I left, I rode to the beach, anxious to release all of the anxiety I'd built up inside of me. Maya was rehearsing with her dance crew tonight. So, I was alone. Left to my own devices, I thought about what I would usually be doing. Hustling, hanging out with Killa Bean and the crew. Instead, I was on my own, watching the sun set on Kingston as I stood by the shore.

I started to dance. I pressed Play on one of Toasta's best mixtapes that I'd downloaded to my phone, discarded my T-shirt and my Timbs, and started practicing the moves Killa Bean and I had created the last time we practiced. It had been days since we choreographed a routine. Days since my mind had been released of all its contents. That's what happened whenever I danced. The harsh reality of my problems melted away, and I became one with the dance. I emptied myself of everything I had been bottling inside. I moved my body until a spirit took over me. I felt inhabited by a force more powerful than I was. I felt swept up in some sort of otherworldly daze as I danced. My legs took on a weightlessness that impressed even me. I knew this was the best I had ever moved in my life. It was like I was in a trance, though I was more aware of myself and my movements than ever before. My dance was powerful, tribal, warrior-like. It felt spiritual. Like a holy force overtook me, and I was moving to the rhythm of an angel's drum. My arms swung like pendulums. My feet moved so swiftly that the sand kicked up around me. With all my heart, I danced.

Caught up in the spirit, I was completely unaware that I was being watched. While I let the music take me over, Kaydeen approached, slowly, observing every motion. She stood there, silently watching me until the song ended, and

I looked around, breathlessly, noticing her presence for the first time.

"Hey," she said, simply.

"Yo." I struggled to catch my breath. "How long you been out here?" I found it simultaneously ironic and eerie that she appeared at a moment when I was in such a spiritual daze.

"Long enough for me to see that you're amazing." She shook her head in awe. "Tarzan, I mean it. Truly amazing. I've never seen anything like that."

I laughed, modestly. I was a bit embarrassed, honestly. I had been so taken over by the dance that I wasn't sure my swag had been up to par.

"How long you been dancing?" she asked.

I shrugged. "About six months."

Her eyes flew wide. "Nah! Ya lie!"

I nodded. "That's the truth."

"You dance like the men I study with at Juilliard. If you auditioned, they would surely give you a scholarship, dancing like that."

I shrugged off her compliments, suddenly shy under her relentless gaze.

"Ya know, it's not a lot of men around here like you. You're special, Tarzan."

I laughed again. "Come on, Kaydeen. You're just trying to blow my head up." I began to sing an old reggae song about being too experienced to be taken for a ride.

"Seriously, Yankee boy!" That smile returned that I loved so much. But, I hadn't forgotten our last encounter.

"Is that why your brother has it out for me and my family?"

She looked away. "I don't know why Donovan does the things he does. He could be intimidated by you."

I agreed. The thought had occurred to me, too.

"When Dada is intimidated by someone he lashes out. That's because he's trying to flip the script. He wants you to be intimidated by him instead."

"Well, I'm not. And, I'm going to show him that he's not the baddest man in the world."

She looked at me. "I told you he would make things miserable for you. I meant what I said. This is only the beginning. Him nah let up."

I laughed. "Well, tell him to keep it coming. Whatever you got, I can handle it."

She shook her head. "What do you mean 'you'? I have nothing to do with it. I want to protect you."

I shot her a glare. "I don't need your protection."

She seemed wounded by that. "Well, even if you don't need me, I won't let him hurt you."

It still felt like she was implying that Dada was more than he truly was.

"He can't hurt me." I looked at her, sincerely, as I said it.

She shook her head again. "I tell him 'no.' But, him wan' kill you."

I laughed. It amused me the way that people spoke about Dada. Like he was the baddest man in the whole land.

"A lot of men have many wants," I said. "But, achieving those goals is an altogether different ting." My attempt at a Jamaican lilt fell short. But, she got the point. "Dada doesn't scare me. That's all you need to know."

"So, the Yankee boy is some kind of badman, eh? Zeen." She nodded, accepting it at last.

"Call it whatever you want. I just live my life without fear. You have to be fearless to get through each day. I learned that back in Brooklyn, by the way. A place a lot worse than Kingston. Just in case you were wondering." I shook my head. Kaydeen had no idea who I was or where I was from. She didn't know that I was capable of far worse than Dada had ever imagined.

"If today is my last, so be it." I looked her dead in the eye. "I ain't scared of nuttin'."

She narrowed her eyes at me like she was trying to figure me out. I realized that Kaydeen wasn't used to encountering guys like me. Here, everyone treated the Davidson family like they were gods. But, I was not impressed by any of their money, power, or prestige. I was Tarzan Brixton, a fearless young nigga from Brooklyn. Not the yardies she was used to.

She stepped closer to me, catching me off guard.

"I like you, Tarzan." I could smell the cinnamon scent on her breath.

I laughed, a bit uneasily. "I like you, too."

She leaned in even closer now. I could feel the heat of her body, as intoxicating as her smile.

"But, you're dangerous," I added.

She recoiled a bit when I said that. Then, to my surprise, she nodded in agreement.

"Ya damn right, I'm dangerous."

My eyes widened. I was pleasantly surprised by her honesty.

"I was under the impression that you like danger," she said. "You have no fear, right?"

I nodded. "No fear." Her body was so close to mine that I could practically feel her nipples pressed against my bare chest. "But, I have a girl." I was reminding Kaydeen, and reminding myself at the same time.

She laughed. "Oh. The sweet little bishop's daughter." She sucked her teeth like she wasn't buying that act.

"That's her," I said. "The woman I love."

"Zeen," she said again. She was learning a lot about me today it seemed. "Well, the woman you love may not be as innocent as ya think. Ya know what dem say. 'Everything that has sugar ain't sweet.'"

I thought about that phrase, and about how it related to Maya. I looked at Kaydeen. Dada's sister. I shook my head. Couldn't trust her point of view.

"Don't hate," I said. "It's not attractive." I took a step back. Suddenly, I realized we were a lot closer than we needed to be.

"Sorry," she said. "I didn't mean to shatter your little image of your sweet likkle girl."

"Don't worry about it. You didn't shatter my image of her at all. You can't. There's nothing you can tell me about Maya that I don't already know."

She looked at me, her eyes dancing. She looked like a woman who loved a challenge.

"Okay. So, I guess she told you all about who she was before she met you."

I thought about that. Sure. Hadn't she? Maya loved dancehall. She was the bishop's daughter, saving herself for her king. She was Peta Gaye's little sister. My baby. I nodded. I knew everything I needed to know.

"She told you how she rolled before she met you?" Kaydeen looked ready to burst at the seams.

I wasn't sure how to respond to that question. It seemed loaded.

Kaydeen sucked her teeth. "Like I said, she wasn't always so sweet. Ya know what they say. That dem church gals are the biggest freaks. Especially a bishop's daughter."

I felt my heart racing. My thoughts turned to making love to Maya, holding her sweet, innocent body in my arms. "What are you talking about?"

Kaydeen frowned a little. "So, you don't know the real reason my brother doesn't like you, nah?"

I stared at her, waiting for her to say more. But, she remained silent.

"Tell me."

She looked like she felt sorry for me. I hated that look more than anything.

"Your sweet little love used to be Dada's girl."

Those words hit me hard, playing on a cruel repeating loop inside my head. My heart shattered into a thousand tiny fragments. I felt hot and like I needed to sit down. I thought of Dada—a man I hated more than anyone—and I thought of Maya. My baby. Against my better judgment, I imagined him touching her, kissing her. I thought of her virginity, and wondered if that had all been a lie. In my head, I thought back to the night I made love to Maya for the first time. I tried to recall the details. Had there been blood on the sheets? Had I felt the barrier break when I entered her? In reality, I had felt like a born-again virgin myself that first time. It had been so long since the last time I had held a woman in my arms. I looked at Kaydeen, my heart crushed. I struggled to find the words to speak, but I came up empty.

"Yeah," she said. "I figured she didn't let you know that,

eh?" The expression on her face was some twisted cocktail of pity and gloating.

I couldn't respond.

Kaydeen touched my arm gently. "I'm not trying to hurt you. I just think you deserve to know the truth. You said you knew everything about Maya. But it's obvious you didn't know that." She shook her head. "I'm not one to break up a happy home. But, you're special, Tarzan. And, I feel like you should be treated as such."

I was speechless.

Kaydeen touched my face. Her hands felt soft against my skin, and it comforted me. I needed some comforting at that moment. Everything I thought I knew about the woman I loved was a lie. I thought about the bishop and the hell he had given me since the moment he met me. I wondered if he had given the same hell to Dada—a man far more evil than I had ever been.

Kaydeen caressed my cheek gently. She leaned in and kissed me. I let her. I completely let go and kissed her back with all the intensity I was feeling. She pulled away moments later. Staring into my eyes, she nodded, slowly.

"Yeah. You're special."

She walked away without another word, leaving me alone with the truth.

I felt like a fool. Just when I thought I had found somebody I could love, it turned out she was a fraud. My mind was wracked by thoughts of Maya with Dada. I imagined him laughing at me when I wasn't even in on the joke. I had finally let my guard down, trusting Maya and giving her my heart. And she had lied to me. Or, at least she hadn't told me the whole truth. Which in my mind was worse. I was vexed.

I thought about leaving Jamaica for good that night. Fuck it, I thought. I could go back to Brooklyn, try to find a job somewhere and start over again. By now things had calmed down, and surely it was safe to return to New York. I had a little money tucked away at Aunt Cheryl's. It was my emergency fund. I had given it to her for safe-keeping when I first started hustling with Farmer. It wasn't much. Just enough for a plane ticket out of town, maybe some new clothes. Back then, I had set the money aside in case I had to get on the move quickly. I thought I might meet some resistance from the other marijuana dealers in the area the way it was back in Brooklyn. I had antici-pated a turf war. But, I never imagined finding myself in the midst of a twisted love triangle that I wasn't even aware I was a part of. Dada had come after me with a vengeance, and it all made sense now. It wasn't just the fact that I was some Yankee boy intruding on his turf. It was the fact that I was loving his girl, taking over what he thought was his dancehall, and doing it all with my usual arrogance.

This wasn't the life I had come to Jamaica searching for. When I got on that plane and left New York, I was running away from my demons, looking for a new start. I thought I'd found that in Maya. In the dancehall. Now, I had to question everything. Part of me was tempted to go home. I could leave now and forget all about the life I had started building here.

But that felt like quitting, which was something I never did. I thought about all the times in my life that I'd been knocked down, only to get back on my feet again. Even when shit looked bleak and utterly impossible, I would press on toward my goal with a stubborn determination. This time would be no different.

I dusted the sand off my clothes, swallowed my pride, and got on my bike. There was no way I was going back to Brooklyn now. Fuck that.

SPELLBOUND

I spent the next few hours getting wasted with some bottles of liquor Uncle Screechie had given me after the raid on his restaurant. He had handed them over hoping they might bring me some comfort from the guilt I'd been feeling. Now that guilt was compounded by the hurt I felt knowing that the woman I loved was a fraud.

Maya still had no idea that I knew the truth. She had already called my cell phone several times, wondering where I was. I was sure the bishop had told her about our conversation at the church earlier. Judging by the desperate voice messages she left on my phone, she was anxious to see me again. But I didn't return the sentiment. Right now, I needed to be alone. I was crushed.

I kept thinking about Dada. I wondered what a man like him—a man with every woman in Jamaica at his disposal—would want with sweet Maya. The woman I knew was regal, full of wisdom and class. Dada was a savage.

"Your sweet little love used to be Dada's girl."

Kaydeen's words still echoed in my mind. I thought of what it would mean, being Dada's girl. Imagining the other side of Maya that must surely exist, I felt like a fool. I thought of my cousin, and wondered why he'd never told me. I felt confused, and the liquor had me feeling anxious.

Eventually, I called my cousin, expecting to find him at home with Peta Gaye and the kids like he said he would be. Instead, I learned that he was at the dancehall. So much for being a man of his word.

I pulled myself together and sobered up enough to ride my motorcycle to the dancehall. I arrived at The Jungle just as it was closing for the night. It was just after four in the morning, and the dancehall parking lot was crowded with people spilling out. Police cars with their lights flashing sat parked outside. People trickled out, their outfits seeming more outrageous than usual at this hour. In the sea of colorful Mohawks, neon outfits, and lots of spandex, I saw my cousin. Toasta walked out of the dancehall holding his equipment and heading for his old rusty car.

I greeted him, and Toasta smiled.

"I thought you were staying home with Peta Gaye tonight," I said.

He shook his head. "Couldn't keep that promise. Casanova said he needed me. Expecting a big crowd tonight and all that. Peta Gaye was pissed, ya hear me?" He shook his head. "But, I'm happy I didn't pass it up. Brethren! Ya missed it. Tonight was a mash-up party!" His eyes were wide just talking about it. "I looked for you all night, expecting you to walk in the door with Killa and the crew."

I shrugged. "I got some more bad news today, believe it or not. Got sidetracked."

Toasta seemed disappointed. "What about all that shit

we was talking 'bout earlier? I thought we were gonna get the crew together again. Get ready for di dance clash. Where ya been?"

"I know, bro." I shook my head. "I need to get my head back in the game. Word."

It was true. I needed to get focused on the right things. What Kaydeen told me had hit me hard. I had been wallowing in my sorrows, drinking, smoking hella weed, and losing time. My mind definitely should have been on dancing. But, I was distracted.

I saw Killa Bean approaching with the rest of the crew. Killa sported a large bandage across his face, courtesy of Dada's enforcers. He wasn't letting it get him down. He already had plans to get a tattoo over the scar Dada's crew had carved into his chest. We popped bottles, and smoked ganja together in the parking lot. For a while, it felt like we had won. Just being there alive despite all that we had already endured, we were victorious.

Killa and the crew rehearsed a dance move while I stood off on the sidelines swigging a bottle of Hennessy. I tucked a bag of weed that Killa had given me down deep inside one of my Timberland boots for later.

I looked over at my cousin, chilling nearby.

"Listen, Toast. I need your ear for a minute."

We stepped away from the crew a bit. Toasta was tearing up some jerk chicken from the food cart.

"I'm bugging out right now," I explained. "We need to talk."

Toasta looked at me, seriously.

"What's wrong? You look like ya got sum'n on your mind."

Indeed I did.

"Yo. Why didn't you tell me that Maya and Dada used to be together?"

His face dropped.

"She nah tell you?"

I looked at him, searching his face for signs of deception. Instead, it was clear that Toasta was genuinely surprised. He shook his head. "Cousin, I thought she tell you a long time ago. Truly."

I shook my head. Part of me still couldn't believe it was true.

"So . . . she was like his *girl*?"

Toasta couldn't look at me. That's when I knew Kaydeen had been telling the truth.

"Listen . . ." Toasta shifted his weight from one foot to the other. "Everyone has a history, brethren. Maya was attracted to the big man 'round town for a likkle bit. But, then she snapped out of it. She must not want to rehash old business."

I gave him a side-eye. "Well, what about Dada? I'm starting to see why he's not so eager to forget the old business between them. And there I am, walking blindly into the whole situation." I sucked my teeth, disgusted by the way the whole thing had played out. No matter how you cut it, I came out looking like the sucker.

Toasta didn't seem sure what to say. He seemed to be processing the secret she had kept from me, and finally understanding my anger.

"Oh, my God. Women can be ruthless, eh?"

The question seemed rhetorical. So I didn't bother to respond.

"Maya Fenster." He gritted his teeth and looked at me sidelong. "I told you that itch was gonna bleed, Tarzan."

I remembered his words to me when I first met Maya. In his own comical way, Toasta had warned me that the Fenster women were a handful. I thought he was referring to the hoops I had to jump through just to get her attention. The dancehall, the bishop, now this. I wished I had known on that sunny day when we first met that Maya had the potential to steal my heart and break it before I even knew what happened.

"Even if you thought I knew, you could have mentioned something about her and Dada."

He looked at me, helplessly. "I thought *she* told you, Tarzan. Look. I got my own relationship problems with her big sister. Peta Gaye is talking about leaving and taking the kids if I don't get a real job. I'm trying to get her to see that my music career is about to jump off. She say she need a man with more stability. Eh? So, forgive me if I didn't pay closer attention to you two."

I felt bad for Toasta. "Man, Peta Gaye ain't going nowhere."

Toasta looked toward the sky like he prayed I was right.

I smiled. "You ain't got nothing to worry about, Toast. You're a good dude. Your dreams are real. They're gonna happen. It's your vision. You believe in it, and I believe in you, bro. Your name is gonna be up in lights. Watch!"

Kaydeen and her Laydeez walked up. I was surprised that they were still hanging around The Jungle at this late/early hour.

"Hey there, Yankee boy," she said. "How are you holding up?"

"I'm fine."

"Ya sure?" She appeared to be mildly amused by my

misfortune. I knew she didn't like Maya. But, right now the last thing I needed was somebody rubbing my nose in it.

"I said I was fine." I took a swig from my bottle of Hennessy.

"Mind if me and mi girls hang out with you until we go home?"

I frowned. "You should be going home now. It's late."

She looked at me, her head tilted to the side, her eyes sexy and captivating.

"Can we stay or not?" She wore her hair in a ponytail, highlighting her flawless facial features. As usual, her dancehall attire was skimpy and she stood there, confidently, with her arms folded across her fluffy breasts.

I smiled involuntarily. "Sure. Why not?"

Her crew blended in with mine, all of us drinking, dancing, laughing in the parking lot. We were having a good time, enjoying each other's company. I found it easy to let my troubles subside whenever Kaydeen was around. It seemed she had a knack for showing up at moments when my mind was flooded with worries. Moments when I found myself at various crossroads with Maya. I watched Kaydeen as she danced and laughed with her friends, joking that I was Tarzan and she was Jane. To me, this woman seemed like a chameleon. At the same time trashy and classy. I wasn't sure why the mixture of those two qualities didn't turn me off. In fact, it was quite the opposite. I felt my dick get hard watching her wind her hips, seductively, in a crop top and skintight leggings.

Suddenly, Kaydeen grabbed my hand, and began dancing with me out of the blue. She turned her back to me, and twerked her booty against me. I was grateful for the barrier between us. Otherwise, I might have forgot where the hell I was, and boned her right there in the parking lot. She was going in! I was confused at first. Until I saw Maya and her crew exiting the club, heading in our direction. Kaydeen leaned back, and ran her hands across my face, her back against my chest, and her ass pressed even tighter against me. She glided her hands down the length of my arms, lingering on the muscles in my biceps. I stood still and let her.

Maya was furious. She charged toward us like a raging bull. When she got close, she stopped, and glared at me with hate in her eyes. She got aggressively close to Kaydeen and addressed both of us with her voice in a clipped tone.

"Um . . . excuse me. Is there something ya wan' tell me?" She looked like she was ready to fight.

I put my sunglasses on and answered her with silence. I knew that if I said anything, it would be disrespectful. Her image in my eyes had been tarnished.

"Tarzan! What di hell is wrong with you?" She looked like she might self-destruct.

I shot a wicked glance in her direction. "I should be asking you the same thing."

She looked from me to Kaydeen and back again.

"What are you talking about, Tarzan? Mi nah have time for ya fuckery!"

I looked at her, amazed by her audacity. After all the shit I had learned about her, she had the nerve to be raising her voice at me.

"Who the hell are you yelling at?" I took a step toward her.

She got in my face. "Mi yell if mi want! You're out here holding hands with this uptown SKETEL!"

Maya screamed the word in Kaydeen's face. It was an old-school Jamaican term for a ghetto tramp. The moment I heard the word, I knew this would end badly. Mama used the word to describe the woman who had run off with my daddy when Trent was just a baby.

The insult hit Kaydeen hard. She let go of me and got right back in Maya's face.

"Who ya call sketel?"

"You! Mi nah stutter!"

Maya mushed Kaydeen, sending her reeling backward until she caught herself. Kaydeen seemed shocked that Maya had laid hands on her. She rushed toward Maya, but I held her back. Both of their crews talked shit on the sidelines, ready for war. Kaydeen's girls, especially, wanted blood.

Kaydeen laughed.

"Funny! Ya wan' call me a sketel when ya never tell di man about you and mi brother."

Maya froze. She looked at me, her eyes filled with guilt.

"Whappem, Maya? Cat got ya tongue? Why did you keep such a crucial piece of information from the man you love?"

Maya looked like she wanted to disappear. She looked at me, her eyes filled with desperation.

"Yeah. You seemed to have left out that little piece of information," I said. "When were you planning on letting me know about your relationship with Dada?"

Maya looked like she had seen a ghost. "I didn't think it mattered, Tarzan." She looked down at her hands. "It was in di foolish past. It doesn't matter."

I laughed. "Apparently, it does. Otherwise, why wouldn't you tell me about it? What happened to honesty, loyalty, and trust? We talked about all those things, remember? You told me I was your first!"

Kaydeen laughed then, and I realized what a fool I looked like to everyone around me. That cut even deeper than Maya's betrayal.

"You were!" Maya insisted.

Kaydeen laughed, louder this time. "Yeah right!"

Before I knew what happened, Maya slapped Kaydeen with all the force in her body. The sound resonated across the parking lot, getting everybody's attention. Immediately, a full-on brawl broke out. Kaydeen's crew and Maya's both jumped into the melee and chaos erupted. Desperately, I tried to tear Maya and Kaydeen apart. But the women were like two feral cats locked in a fight so vicious that I feared for my own safety.

I heard Dada's jarring voice before I saw him.

"Well, well, well! What do we have here?"

Kaydeen and Maya finally withdrew to separate corners. Both of them were still angry. Especially Kaydeen. She called out from behind a wall of her friends.

"Miss Perfect didn't tell Tarzan about her history with you, brother." She laughed, wickedly. "All this time, Tarzan didn't know."

Dada looked at me, smiling.

"Looks like someone finally found out the truth, eh? A likkle Jamaican history for ya, huh, Yankee boy? Look. Mi nah sweat it. Every hoe have their history. Mi nah wan' her no more. You can have that bitch."

It happened without any thought whatsoever. I punched

Dada across his face so hard that his sunglasses flew off. Stunned, he stumbled backward, and before he could gather himself, I cracked my Hennessy bottle hard across his head.

Dada fell to the ground in a motionless heap.

His crew rushed in and complete anarchy ensued. Fists, knives, machetes, chains all came out in a wild frenzy of rage. All of us were locked in a battle to the death, and I felt the cold steel of a knife slicing through my arm. I recoiled to find Kutan barreling down on me with his machete raised at a deadly angle. Killa Bean appeared then, rushing Kutan, and knocking him to the ground with such force that Kutan dropped his weapon. Killa busted him in the head with the handle of his own machete, ensuring that Dada's enforcer would be sleeping for a long time. Suddenly a gunshot rang out amidst all the ruckus, and I turned to see Dada standing with his gold-plated gun in the air. I wasn't sure when he had regained consciousness, or how much time had passed while we were locked in this bloody battle. His eyes scanned the crowd, frantically, searching. In my gut, I knew he was trying to spot me.

Within seconds, the police swarmed the scene. Everybody scattered.

I jumped on my motorcycle and revved the engine. Kaydeen jumped on the back of my bike just as I prepared to pull off.

"I'm with you," she said, breathlessly.

I hesitated a second before gunning the engine. She held on tightly to me as I sped away from the scene.

We rode along the coastline, the scenery even more magnificent than usual as the sun rose on the shoreline.

I wasn't sure why Kaydeen had decided to come with me. It didn't matter. I needed an escape so desperately. It was hard to imagine how I would get myself out of the mess I'd made this time. Once again, I had let my anger get the best of me. I knew there would be hell to pay in the days to come. But, tonight I decided not to worry about any of that. The more distance we put between us and the dancehall, the better I felt. I felt light as a feather, with Kaydeen pressed firmly against my back as we rode out.

We left Kingston and headed out to Portland. Kaydeen suggested it. She said it would be safe if we rode out to the coast where her father had a manor. She wanted to show me a different side of Jamaica.

"It'll help clear your mind," she said in my ear as we rode together.

I didn't fight it. I wanted to get as far away from everyone and everything that I knew as possible. Maya. The bishop. Dada. Everybody. I felt like I was suffocating. A change of scenery sounded nice.

We arrived at the manor just after sunrise. She showed me around the impressive property. I took it all in as best I could. My eyes felt heavy, as if I was high off of Farmer's best weed. Still, I let her lead me around on a tour of the place. It was a large home with what seemed like a dozen bedrooms. I wanted to be more excited about it. But, the truth was I was exhausted. I fell asleep in one of the guest rooms within minutes after we arrived.

When I woke up hours later, Kaydeen was right by my side. Her hair was fanned out on the pillow beneath her. She looked like an angel lying there asleep beside me. She woke up a few minutes after I did, her eyes dancing again.

"You're awake now, eh, Sleeping Beauty?" She winked. "You talk in your sleep," she said.

I frowned. I worried about what she might have heard. With everything I had on my mind, there was no telling what I uttered. "What was I saying?"

"Apparently, there's some place that you don't want to go back to." She touched me tenderly on my cheek. "You kept saying that in your sleep. 'I don't want to go back.'"

I nodded. I knew exactly what that was about. Prison. The thought of it had been haunting me ever since I emerged from the jail in Kingston. Now more than ever, with the threat of Dada breathing down my neck like an evil dragon, I worried that I might be pushed to make decisions that would force me right back to the place I never wanted to see again.

Kaydeen didn't press the issue, and I was grateful. She sat up in the bed and faced me, her smile bright.

"Come with me," she said. "I want to show you something."

I followed her, encouraged by her enthusiasm as she led me downstairs. Now that I was wide awake, I looked around at the grounds of the plantation-style manor she had brought me to. The place was lavish. The furnishings were old, solid wood. It all looked antique, sophisticated, and expensive. I reminded myself that the woman I'd gotten to know on the gritty floor of the dancehall was a wealthy and privileged socialite who lived in a world I knew nothing about.

I was impressed by how she managed to navigate those two worlds so seamlessly. If I had met her in the circles of New York's arts and culture scene, I would have been im-

pressed by the beautiful dancer with an international flair.
If I had encountered her in the ritzy world she gave me a
tour of now, it would have been easy to see that she was
comfortable and very well versed as she fluttered among
the finest things money could buy. But, instead, I had met
her in the rawness and savage bestial energy of The Jungle. Kaydeen seemed to morph from dancehall queen to
sophisticated jet-setter in the blink of an eye.

She brought me outside and led me down a long, winding trail in the back of the big house. It was a gorgeous day
in Jamaica. Like something out of a fairy tale. The sky was
so blue and clear, and the lush green gardens seemed to reso-
nate with scents and colors. The path was obscured by trees,
and the sun played peekaboo between the branches. It felt
romantic, walking with Kaydeen along that path, headed for
an unknown destination. She held my hand, gently, as we
walked. Soon, we arrived at an amazing waterfall on the far
end of the property. It was the most breathtaking thing I
had ever seen.

Without a word, she stripped down to her bathing suit.
It was skimpy to say the least. A tiny string bikini that left
absolutely nothing to the imagination. It was impossible
not to stare, and hard not to drool as she dipped her toe into
the streaming water. She jumped back, giggling at the cold
temperature against her flawless skin. My eyes were locked
on the way her chest bounced as she leaped. The jiggle of
her ass and thighs with every step she took. This girl was
bad and she knew it.

She dove into the water and swam around beneath the
surface before coming back up for air. I watched her, impressed by her form.

"Come in!" she called out to me.

I peeled off my shirt and dove in without hesitation. The water was cold, but it didn't take me long to adjust. Kaydeen moved in close to me, our bodies warming one another beneath the water. We swam together, chasing each other playfully and splashing around. Kaydeen was gorgeous, fun, and free-spirited. She seemed to be feeling me, too, judging by the way she touched me every chance she got. She couldn't keep her hands off me, and I wasn't complaining. We bonded that day, blocking out all of the drama that had surrounded us in the days before. Finally, we climbed out of the water and dried off in the sunshine. I leaned against a large rock beneath the waterfall and caught my breath.

Kaydeen looked at me and smiled. Then she began to dance for me, grinning as she winded her hips. I smiled, too, enjoying the show. I had forgotten all about Maya, about the beef I had with Dada, and everything else that had been troubling me. Instead of burying my head in my hands, I danced with Kaydeen beneath the waterfall on a perfect sunny day in Jamaica. I felt freer than I had in years.

I took her in my arms, and pulled her close, grinding into her to a rhythm only we could hear. I kissed her with my hands cupping her face firmly. I needed her to feel what I was feeling. How desperately I meant that kiss. Kaydeen moaned with pleasure, and she held on to me tightly.

Boldly, she grabbed my manhood in her hands as she kissed me. I was hard as a missile. She stroked me until I was on the verge of erupting. Her grip was firm, contrasted by the softness of her delicate hands. This felt better than anything I had ever experienced in my life. Better than Tameka, better than Maya.

Maya.

I pulled away for some reason. Aware, perhaps, that what was going down between me and Kaydeen was wrong. She didn't let me go, though. Instead, she released her beautiful, perfect breasts from her bikini top, dropped to her knees, and took me into her mouth.

My head rolled back in complete ecstasy. My hands wandered without my consent. The sound of the pounding waterfall, the feeling of Kaydeen's mouth on me, her breasts in my hands. It was all too much. My knees buckled as I erupted in her mouth. Instead of recoiling, she kept going, slowing her pace, and sucking every drop as it poured forth from me like a geyser. I gasped for air, experiencing a feeling unlike anything I had ever experienced before.

I felt like my head exploded, in more ways than one. I sat on the ground beneath the waterfall afterward, spent.

Kaydeen sat beside me, her head resting gently on my shoulder. She seemed relaxed and unfazed by what had just occurred, or by my reaction to it.

"Have you ever seen anything so beautiful?" She was talking about the waterfall. But, she could easily have been speaking of herself. At that moment, she looked like the most stunning woman I'd ever seen.

"It's definitely something," I said. I felt like I was dreaming. All of this felt too good to be true. Surreal. I glanced at Kaydeen, wondering if she was feeling as strange as I was.

"Totally different from Kingston, eh?"

I nodded. "Yeah. Definitely." I took a deep breath and let it out slowly. "I needed this more than you know. Thank you." I was thanking her for more than just the tour of Portland. She had just blown my mind.

"You don't have to thank me," she said. "Like I told you, you're special to me. I want to take care of you." She chuckled. "Even though you're stubborn and won't let me."

I grinned. For a moment I felt a twinge of guilt at the thought of Maya. She would be devastated if she knew what happened between Kaydeen and me beneath that waterfall. Although she had lied to me, I still loved her. Maya was still the woman I had imagined spending the rest of my life with.

But, Kaydeen was putting in a hard bid for my affection. It was tough to ignore the fact that the woman beside me was a stunning beauty, built like a brickhouse, with a fortune in her bank account. I imagined myself as her man. It sounded good. But, we both knew there was more to the story than that.

"I think your brother is the one that won't let that happen." She didn't argue. "I look at you sometimes and it bugs me out. You have an air about you that makes it hard to imagine that you and Dada are cut from the same cloth. You seem so different from him." I couldn't understand it. The more time I spent with her, the harder it was for me see the two of them in the same light. "You're sweet. Sexy. Smart. Are you sure you two are related?"

Kaydeen laughed. "Different mothers. Same father. Who is an amazing man, I might add." She lit up at the mention of her father.

"Yeah," I said. "I've heard a lot about him." I recalled the things that Toasta and Maya had told me about the ruthlessness of Pierce Davidson. I definitely understood how Dada could descend from such a sickening legacy.

She looked at me. "Not the folklore. Not the Big Babylon bakra they make him out to be. I'm talking about my sweet, loving father. You should meet him."

I balked at that. "Nah. I'm good." I shook my head. "I don't do well with fathers. The tattoos, the Yankee attitude. I don't think I'll be the ideal choice for the type of guy his daughter brings home to meet him."

She took my hands in hers, leaned in, and kissed me. With her hands in mine, our lips pressed together, and our tongues doing a slow, erotic dance, I felt hypnotized once more by Kaydeen's allure. At that moment, she could have honestly asked me for anything and I would have given in.

She pulled away from our kiss, breaking her spell at last. Or so I thought.

"You're meeting him. Now. Let's go."

Like a sheep, I followed her lead

BLACK MAGIC

I t was clear that the palace Kaydeen brought me to was far removed from the belly of the beast that was the Kingston dancehall scene. Not just far away in terms of geography. It was miles apart in terms of the quality of life. Even the air felt cleaner up here. We ventured up to a cliff-side manor. It was the type of fancy home that my mama might have bragged about cleaning during the odd jobs she had taken as a domestic worker over the years. Now I understood why Kaydeen had brought me to Portland. Her father's massive mansion was like stepping into another world.

We were way up in the hillside, the property miles away from their closest neighbors. Gates surrounded the perimeter of the massive plot of land. Once inside, we rode for several minutes before the road we were on led into a large circular drive in front of a towering house. As we pulled up on my motorcycle, I was awestruck. I had never been invited to a home this large on grounds this sprawling. The mansion itself was unbelievable. Large picture windows, impossibly high ceilings, marble everything. The place had an old English décor, and an unavoidable echo in each huge room.

As we entered, Kaydeen called out, "Father! Father!" Her voice reverberated throughout the mansion. I saw several staff members milling about. Some were cleaning, others rushing from one room to the next. Each of them avoided making eye contact with us as much as possible. I couldn't stop staring. All of them were dark-skinned black people wearing old-fashioned maid's uniforms, bonnets, and unhappy grimaces. I felt like I had stepped back in time in the worst way. I imagined this had once been an old slave master's plantation, filled with black people hustling around to bend, serve, and cower. I locked eyes with one of them, an old woman whose smooth brown skin bore the tale of many losses. She wore a black maid's uniform with a crisp white apron tied over the top of it. She stared at me, and seemed to be giving me some type of warning with her eyes. They were wide, as if she were trying to tell me something. A sense of complete dread flooded my body; the threat of imminent danger was present. For a moment, I was distracted by the woman, so much that I felt paralyzed by an irrational sense of fear. Suddenly, I felt like I never should have come here. I looked around, hoping to find an excuse to leave—until Kaydeen took me by the hand and led me into the great room. The moment her hand touched mine, a wave of reassuring calm washed over me.

Still, I was intimidated and a bit uncomfortable as we waited for her father to come. This was definitely an unfamiliar environment for me. The place felt cold, steely. I wondered what it was like for her to grow up in a home so formal and uptight.

Her father appeared at the top of the stairs. I looked up at him, imagining him as the subject of all the stories I'd been told. He wasn't very tall. But, his demeanor was authoritative. Much like the bishop, he had an air of importance about him I could feel even from a distance. He was smiling down at us, his eyes focused on me. I stared back at him. Pierce Davidson, in the flesh. He had pale skin and dark hair, and wore a well-fitted suit. I had heard so much about him that seeing him now felt a little surreal. He greeted us, and began descending the large spiral staircase toward where we stood. He reached the bottom and hugged his daughter tightly.

I checked him out. Like his son, he looked to me like an average white guy who was too cocky for his own good. He smelled good, though. I pictured him flying to Dubai just to buy whatever expensive cologne he had on.

Kaydeen introduced us. I shook his hand, and he gave me a smile that made it clear where Kaydeen's charm came from.

"Tarzan! Kaydeen has told me so much about you."

My smile faded a little. I didn't really like the sound of that. I wasn't sure why she would be talking to her father about me. I glanced at Kaydeen. She avoided making eye contact with me, focusing instead on her father.

"Daddy, I spent the morning hanging out with Tarzan here. And, over the course of our conversation, I mentioned you. Of course, I found myself rambling about what a wonderful father you are, and all of that. So, instead of talking about you, I brought him to meet you in person." She looked at me, beaming.

"It's a pleasure to meet you," Mr. Davidson continued. "I'm happy I was here to meet you this afternoon. I've just returned late last evening from the cold and gray city of London." He made a face as if he was nauseous. "Such a boring and unemotional city. Anyway, I'm happy to be home once again. I invite you to stay for dinner. My staff has just finished preparing it. Please. Join me. It will be an honor."

He had an accent I couldn't place. It was partly British, part Jamaican, and maybe a few others thrown in for good measure. I wasn't sure what to make of him. He seemed odd and eccentric. Maybe a little crazy. He waved his hands and staff members rushed about, I assumed in order to prepare a place for me at the table. I opened my mouth to politely decline. But, already, Pierce was talking about his flight from London, and his plans to travel again at the end of the week.

Like his daughter, Pierce Davidson had a way of sweeping me up in a trance. At some point during the fast-moving conversation, I must have agreed to his invitation. Because before I knew it, he was ushering Kaydeen and me into a dining room unlike any one I'd ever been in before. It was huge in size and waitstaff dressed in crisp, starched uniforms lined the walls. It felt like a scene out of the antebellum South, and I tried hard not to stare at their faces. Surely, being lined up this way like slaves waiting to call on their master was demeaning enough. The long table in the center of the room was set for a full-course meal. I could see that Pierce Davidson lived a life fit for a king.

He took a seat at the head of the table. Kaydeen sat to his right, and motioned for me to sit down opposite her. Flanking her father now, we sat awkwardly while the staff tended to us, filling our glasses with water and a wine so red and thick that it looked like blood. Unfamiliar with such a formal environment, I waited, unsure. I watched Kaydeen, and followed her movements. Placing my napkin in my lap, choosing the correct fork for the first course, all of this was new to me. I did my best not to stick out like a sore thumb.

Pierce raised his glass in a toast. Kaydeen and I followed suit. The large glass was nearly full, and I reminded myself that I had better sip slowly. I didn't want to get drunk.

"To my pulchritudinous daughter and her new friend, Mr. Brixton."

I wondered what the hell that word meant. "Pulchritudinous." I couldn't even pronounce that shit. It sounded insulting, but I doubted he would disrespect his daughter. I made a mental note to Google it later.

Kaydeen was beaming. "Thank you, father." They sipped their wine. I did, too. The wine hit my taste buds and I resisted the urge to gag. This one had a strong, bold flavor. Like it was more potent than a typical wine. I frowned at my glass as I set it down.

Pierce clapped his hands together, loudly, startling me. "Please, let's eat!"

The staff rushed in with a flourish, serving the food and uncovering heaping dishes of foods I didn't recognize. I prayed there would be some rice or provisions I could eat. But, there was no such luck. Instead, as the staff uncovered each dish my stomach sank. There was a thick cut of some mystery meat I had definitely never seen before. It looked like a lamb chop, but was far thicker, meatier, and slightly bloody. Nothing about it looked appetizing. The only thing accompanying it on my plate was a drizzle of some brown-ish orange glaze. Or maybe it was gravy. I wasn't sure. I tried not to gag at the sight of it all.

"So, Mr. Brixton. My daughter tells me you are from Brooklyn." Pierce was smiling at me as he spoke. He looked excited to talk to me.

"Yes, sir." I cut into the meat on my plate and a long stream of blood trickled out. I groaned inside. Aware that Pierce was still watching me, I smiled and forced myself to take a bite. The meat was gummy, thick, and unseasoned. I wanted to throw up, but forced myself not to. I took a sip of wine to wash it down, and regretted that immediately. I wasn't sure which tasted worse.

"I have some property in Brooklyn," Pierce said. "It's an interesting place now. All it needed was a little polish." He smiled, seeming quite pleased with himself.

I hated the "new" Brooklyn. Full of yuppies, juice bars, and gentrified neighborhoods. I preferred the old-school Brooklyn. The one Biggie rose from to become the king of New York. I stared at my plate, not wanting to argue with Kaydeen's father on the subject.

"I also hear that you are quite the attraction in Kingston." He managed to still smile while he chewed.

I looked at him, unsure of what he was saying with his odd way of talking.

"At the dancehall," he added, clarifying it for me.

I nodded. "Yes, sir." I supposed I was. I wondered how much he had heard about me. And whether some of what he heard had come from his other child. Again, I felt the now familiar sense of danger lurking close by.

"Father, Tarzan is prepared to win the ten-million-dollar

dance clash tomorrow night. He and his crew are the best. You really should see them for yourself. Some of their moves are more like acrobatics than dance. It's amazing." Kaydeen sounded like a completely different person in the presence of her father. I stared at her in awe.

Pierce chewed his food like it was the most delicious meal he'd ever eaten. I wondered why my taste buds were responding so differently. He smiled at me, a hint of mischief in his gaze.

"Ten million dollars is a nice little prize. Good pocket change." He chugged his wine.

I tried to ignore his condescending tone and attempted to eat some more of the fancy food instead. But, Pierce pressed on.

"I was never one for the . . . shall we call it, the 'allure' of the Kingston club scene. Even in my youth, I found nothing about it appealing."

I looked at him. Now, he was firing too many shots.

"You know, if I grew up in a lifestyle this lavish, I would probably feel the same way you do. But, I'm from the 'hood. I grew up in a place just like Kingston. So, to me, the dancehall scene feels right at home."

Pierce didn't answer me. Instead, he stared, contemplating me in stunned silence.

Kaydeen tried to fill the void. "Tarzan is being modest, father." She chuckled, nervously. "His family is from Hellshire. You've probably heard of the place."

My eyes shot in her direction. I wondered if that was a sly way of eluding to Maya's past with Dada. She winked at me, still smiling. "Tarzan is from humble beginnings, but he has a regal comportment."

Pierce nodded. "It is good to be humble."

Kaydeen reached across the table and patted my hand sweetly.

Pierce watched, grinning at us. "You know," he said. "You two remind me of an old Jamaican folktale. It was one that my nanny used to tell me. Have you ever heard of Anansi, Mr. Brixton?"

I shook my head. "No, sir." I was grateful for the distraction from the interesting concoction on the plate in front of me.

He nodded. "Anansi is like the Jamaican Spider-Man. He is, literally, a super spider that symbolized hope to Jamaicans. Anansi was the oppressed people's hero. Yet, he wasn't perfect."

Pierce noticed that I wasn't eating, and he stopped talking and gestured at my plate. "Please, eat."

I did, forcing the food down while I listened. My stomach churned again, and I prayed that no one heard it but me.

"Anansi was both the fool and the fooler." He laughed at his own made-up word. "The high god's accomplice and his rival. An irresistible and indestructible spider whose tales have been passed down for centuries."

Kaydeen chewed her food, seeming thrilled by her father's storytelling. She looked at me. "Father would tell me the tales of Anansi every night at bedtime when I was a little girl."

I smiled, took another sip of wine, and vowed silently to myself that I wouldn't eat another piece of that mystery meat, no matter what.

Pierce stood up from the table and began pacing the room while he continued to tell his story. It caught me off guard. We were in the middle of a meal and there he was walking around the room like a character in a Hitchcock movie. I glanced at Kaydeen, but she seemed unfazed. Like she was used to her father's theatrics and didn't find them strange at all.

"One of my favorite stories is about Anansi and the king's daughter. It's a fine tale."

He lit a pipe filled with God knows what, and the scent of it mixed in with the smell of the food and the effects of the wine. The combination made my head spin.

"Long ago, Anansi heard that the king's daughter was a riddle master."

Kaydeen giggled at that. I smiled, hoping my face wasn't betraying how tipsy I felt. The room felt like it was spinning around on its axis.

"She was gorgeous, intelligent, and in her leisure time she loved to solve riddles. The king's daughter proclaimed that whoever should give her a riddle that she could not solve, that man would be her husband, and later king!"

Pierce took a puff on his pipe, and faced me. He began walking slowly in my direction as he continued telling the story.

"But, if she guessed the riddle, the man's head must be cut off."

He stared at me for so long that I thought he must expect me to respond. I opened my mouth to speak, but nothing came out. I frowned, and tried to force some sound out. Still nothing. I looked at him. Pierce grinned and continued pacing, the smoke from his pipe drifting skyward.

"Anansi was up for the challenge. He told his mother that he would make up a riddle on his journey to meet the princess and he would deliver it to her and become the new king. Anansi's mother was leery of this mission. She worried for her son. But, being a spiritual woman, she allowed him to set out on his mission. For his journey, Anansi's mother gave him some magic dumplings. Seven in total. She gave to him six healthy dumplings. But she poisoned one of them."

The room had stopped swirling now. But, Pierce's voice sounded like a record that had been slowed down so that the voice was distorted. I looked at Kaydeen, but she seemed out of focus. I blinked my eyes and tried to clear them. Pierce kept right on talking.

"On the journey, Anansi ate five dumplings and he gave two of the dumplings to the donkey he was riding. One of the two was the poisoned dumpling. The poor donkey died on the journey. A raven flying above ate the dead donkey's carcass and was poisoned, too. The raven died, landing in a hog farm. The hogs ate the poisoned raven and two of the hogs were contaminated and died. The hogs were made into food that fed the entire town, except for the kingdom, of course. The whole town suffered a plague and was completely wiped out. The only people who survived were Anansi, still on his journey, and the men and women in the king's court. The upper echelon, affluent folk. Somewhat like the uptowners in Kingston, I might say."

He chuckled at his own joke. I did, too, although my laugh was slightly delayed and a little louder than I had meant for it to be. My voice was back now, and I was shocked to hear it again. I was really trying to pull myself together. But this food, the wine, or both had me feeling loopy.

"So, as the story goes, Anansi over time finally gets to

the palace. He gives the king's daughter the riddle of his journey. He says to her, 'One poisoned none, yet poisoned all. For the mighty to partake amongst the meek, the kingdom shall fall.'"

Pierce took one long inhale of his pipe. He exhaled and laughed.

I was confused. I figured I must have missed something. I hadn't been listening very closely. Not with everything I was feeling at the moment. It felt like I had just downed an entire bottle of Hennessy, smoked a blunt to the head, and took a snort of cocaine back to back. I forced myself to focus on Kaydeen's father. But, on the inside I was yearning for my bed and my mama.

"I'm sorry, Mr. Davidson. I'm not sure if I understand the riddle."

"Neither did the king's daughter."

I waited for him to say more. He sat silent.

I thought about the parts of the story I had managed to comprehend. My curiosity was piqued.

"So, did Anansi become king or was he killed?"

Pierce snapped his head in my direction. His face was stretched wide in a twisted sneer. He looked like a villain in a movie. Only this was real life. Or at least I thought it was. It was hard to tell what was real and what was imagined through the fog inside my head.

"Find out the answer to that riddle, Tarzan. And you will find out the answer to your question."

I looked at Kaydeen, confused. She stared back at me and shrugged her shoulders. I figured she was as lost as I was.

I cleared my throat. "Well, thank you for dinner and

that interesting story, Mr. Davidson." My mouth felt cottony, and dry. I licked my lips, which only made it worse.

"All my pleasure, Mr. Brixton. I shall retire to my study now. I have a few business meetings in the morning. Good night, Kaydeen. Mr. Anansi."

I looked at him, and he gave me a wink. The smirk on his face was unsettling as he shook my hand and kissed his daughter good night. He left, and the staff immediately began clearing the table.

I looked at Kaydeen.

"Wow," I said. "Your father is really an interesting man."

She nodded. "Yes. My father is a very wise man. I've learned a lot from him." She stood up. "Come. I live here on the property as well. Let me show you where my villa is."

I managed to rise from the table, slowly. The effects of that wine had me a little wobbly. But, Kaydeen didn't seem to notice. She looped her arm through mine and walked me outside. We strode together through a neat, manicured garden to a home in the middle of the Davidson estate and she ushered me inside. I looked around at the spacious house.

"Is it cool for me to be in here with you so late?" My words were flowing easier now. I was relieved. "Maybe I should hop on my bike and head back to Kingston. I don't need your father coming in here and hitting me with some more deadly riddles."

She laughed.

"Settle down, Tarzan. You're fine. He's all the way up in the big house. He never comes down this way. Besides, I'm a grown woman."

"Oh, really?"

She grinned, seductively. "Really. And I like to do grown

woman tings." She slipped her dress off, slowly. Now she stood before me wearing nothing but the bottom of her string bikini.

The warrior between my legs saluted her incredible body. She stepped toward me, her eyes locked onto mine. I felt transported outside of myself. Like I was watching her move toward me in slow motion. She reached where I stood and kissed me, her hands roaming all over my body. The sensation of her lips against my skin felt prickly and strange. Then, without warning it felt sensual and erotic. My head was spinning again. I needed to sit down.

Kaydeen sucked tenderly on my lower lip, her hands rubbing my chest, arms, head. I squeezed her breasts, toying with her until she moaned in pleasure. I looked at her face, and my mind began playing tricks on me. Suddenly, it wasn't Kaydeen in my arms any longer. It was Maya.

Maya stood with her cocoa-brown skin shining in the light. My queen. So beautiful and sweet. Her eyes were closed, her head tilted back, and her face twisted into the most erotic and sensual expression I had ever seen. She looked like she was about to come, her lips parted breathlessly. I put my hand inside of her panties and slid my finger inside of her tight, wet walls.

"Maya," I whispered.

She tensed up. "Excuse me?"

Her reaction stunned me. I looked at her, dazed. I shook my head, trying to clear my vision and make the room come into clearer focus somehow.

"Maya," I said again.

"What about her?" Kaydeen stepped back, and pushed my hand away. She seemed angry.

I could see a little clearer now. The fog in my mind slowly began to dissipate, and I realized where I was. *I shouldn't be here.* I looked at Kaydeen standing practically naked before me, and knew I'd made a big mistake.

"I love her," I said. "I can't do this."

Kaydeen stepped forward again. "Of course you can." She attempted to kiss me again, and I pushed her away.

"I can't," I said. "I need to go." I stepped toward the door, but she blocked me.

She looked furious. "So you g'wan turn all of this down?"

She motioned toward her perfect body. I understood her disbelief. Any heterosexual man in his right mind would have been inside of her by now. But, I wasn't in my right mind. I was in love with Maya. As crazy as that was, it stopped me from crossing that line. The old me would have dived right in. Especially with all the secrets and lies Maya had allowed to come between us. But, that old me was gone. Now, I wanted to get out of there and get back to Kingston.

"Do you know how many men would die to be here with me right now?" Her voice was raised, and she was talking with her hands and twisting her neck in universal black girl fashion.

I nodded. I'm sure there were many. "Maybe you should call one of them." I stepped toward the door again, but she advanced on me. She moved closer and attempted to kiss me again. I resisted.

"Come on, Kaydeen. This ain't right." I tried to step around her. She blocked my exit. "Step back! I'm not playing!" My voice was louder than I meant for it to be. But, I was getting frustrated. I knew now, more than ever, that I should not be there. Not on the grounds of the Davidson estate in Kaydeen's personal living quarters. Not with Dada looking for me to settle countless scores.

"Maybe you should just man up!" She yelled at me loudly. It seemed to snap her out of attack mode. At least a little. She moved toward me, slower this time. "I see the potential in you, Tarzan. Come on. You don't have to front for me." She gestured at the luxurious fruits of her father's cruel labor. "Mi know ya rather live like this than to be stuck down there in the pit of Kingston with Maya and di bishop."

I shook my head. "I love her. That's what you're not understanding."

"Love?" She laughed. "That is child's play. Mi nah juvenile like them other gals you're used to dealing with. I don't care who you love. I don't care if you have other women. I just want you."

I stepped back, amazed by what I was hearing. She stepped forward, closing the distance between us.

"Men will be men, Tarzan. That's the way it is. So just be a man."

I thought I must be insane, turning her down. This gorgeous woman was giving me a free pass to sleep with her, and to continue sleeping with Maya and anyone else that I saw fit. It was all too good to be true. And that's what I realized as I looked at her, and listened to the words she was uttering. It was the same feeling I had gotten since the first moment I laid eyes on her. Everything about Kaydeen Davidson—her beauty, her wealth, her power, and her promises—was just too good to be true.

I pulled away from her one final time. I held my arms out in front of me defensively.

"You're right," I said. "That's exactly what I'm gonna do. I'm gonna be a man." I walked toward the door.

Kaydeen grabbed my shirt as I tried to leave. I yanked away, forcefully, trying to get free.

"Get off of me!"

The force of my movement sent her flying to the floor hard. I apologized right away for shoving her so hard. I hadn't meant to hurt her. But, she wasn't trying to hear me. I tried to help her to her feet and she stubbornly swatted my hand away. I realized that she was angrier about the fact that I was leaving than she was about the push.

She glared at me. Her eyes, usually so alive and full of wonder, were now fiery darts aimed right in my direction. "No one tells me no!" She was yelling so loudly that her voice echoed in the room.

I twisted my face up, disgusted. I hated women who thought they were too good to hear that word. Flashbacks of Tameka made me shudder. "I just did." I moved toward the door again. This time, she couldn't stop me.

"You're going to regret this, Tarzan." She was breathing so heavily that her chest was heaving.

I rushed out the door and started walking across the grounds toward where my motorcycle was parked. I prayed I was going in the right direction. She had taken me on such a twisty path at a time I was under the spell of whatever wild concoction she and her father had given me. I quickened my pace, looking for signs I was heading the right way. I could sense that I needed to get out of there fast. My head still felt foggy, but the fresh air made me feel clearer now. Suddenly, I heard Kaydeen's screaming behind me, her voice cutting through the peace and quiet on the large estate.

"FATHER! FATHER! HELP ME! HE'S RAPED ME!"

My heart was pounding as I began to run toward my motorcycle. Kaydeen kept screaming, and I was sure someone heard her cries. I had to get the hell out of there fast. I heard voices and the sounds of someone running far behind me. I kept running, faster now, in disbelief that Kaydeen would take this shit so far. I jumped on my bike and sped away from the estate, aware that I was the most wanted man in Kingston.

SANCTUARY

I rode through the night, hiding out at odd spots along the roadside to rest from time to time. I managed to doze off a little, parking my bike behind tall bushes while I propped my back against the base of a palm tree and slept. My sleep was understandably fitful, though. I was paranoid that every snapping twig was the sound of my pursuers discovering me. I set out early in the morning and arrived at the bishop's church just after sunrise. He was alone in his office, studying the Bible and preparing a sermon.

He looked up as I stepped inside.

"I figured I would hide out in the last place anyone would look for me." I glanced around at the church sanctuary, bathed in fresh sunlight pouring in through the stained glass windows. Something about the place felt so comforting. I could almost hear my mother's whispered prayers as I stood there. A warm spirit of peace surrounded me. Even I had to appreciate the irony. Godless Tarzan Brixton seeking asylum from a bishop in a Christian church.

Bishop looked at me and offered a weak smile. With his hand, he waved me in. I stepped farther inside.

"Mr. Brixton. What brings you here? Let me guess. More trouble?" His words had their usual bite, but his face seemed relaxed, maybe even welcoming.

I stepped closer.

"No, sir," I answered, sarcastically. "Just thought I would come and check in with you," I joked. "You and your righteous God. I've been calling Him lately, you know? Quite a few times, actually. But, He's not picking up. So, here I am. Figured I'd stop by His house and see if He was home."

Bishop chuckled. It was one of the few times I'd seen him smile. "That's a good one. But, something tells me that you are in no position to be joking right now." He looked at me seriously. "I got a call about you late last night. Tarzan, I have told you this before. It's not safe for you to be here."

I sat down. I was exhausted from running all night. My shoulders were slumped and I looked as defeated as I felt.

"It's never been safe for me to be anywhere, Bishop."

He stared at me. "There are serious allegations against you, Tarzan. The entire Kingston police force is searching for you. Kaydeen Davidson is saying that you raped her last night."

I closed my eyes as I heard those words. I wished I could go back and erase my actions over the past twenty-four hours. That evil, coldhearted bitch was lying on me. I shook my head in disbelief.

Bishop's expression told me that he believed what he'd heard.

"When I got the call, the first thing I thought was that

I should have left you in jail." His expression was cold and emotionless now.

I shook my head again.

"Bishop, I know you don't really care for me. I walk around here in my Timberland boots, my Yankees baseball cap, and my arrogance. No father would want that for his daughter. I've managed to get myself in my share of trouble lately. But, you have to know in your heart that I would never do something like this. I would *never* rape a woman. I am not this demon that you keep making me out to be."

"I'm not the one bringing these charges against you, young man. This trouble is of your own making." He stared out the window for a moment. "I prayed about it," he said. "And the Lord gave me this passage. Exodus 23:7. You know what it says?"

I shook my head, unapologetically. "Nope."

"'Keep far from a false matter and be very careful not to condemn to death the innocent and the righteous, for I will not justify and acquit the wicked.'"

I let that settle in.

"You were right, Tarzan. When you referred to church folk as hypocrites. Sometimes we can be."

I was shocked. I never expected the bishop to admit that.

He sighed. He seemed as weary as I was at the moment.

"My wife used to say that I was a stubborn old churchman who only sees things through the lens of the good book." He held up his Bible for emphasis. "She accused me of only seeing life in black and white, never leaving room for any gray areas. When you stormed out of my car the other day, I told my daughter that I never wanted her to see you again. 'The boy is *lost*,' I said. I urged her to wash her hands of you. But, then I saw a sadness descend over her unlike anything I'd seen before. She sees something in you that I do not see. I have finally accepted that there may be a side of you that I haven't given myself a chance to get to know."

He nodded. "After Maya followed you, that day, I remembered that I am a man of God. I am called to redeem the lost, not to condemn. I was wrong. I may have judged you and I apologize for that."

I nodded. "It's all good, Bishop." I laughed, uneasily. This wasn't going to be easy to admit. "Listen . . . If Maya were my daughter I wouldn't want her to be with a man like me, either. I'm a trouble magnet, always knee-deep in some nonsense. The minute I get myself out of one disaster, I find myself right in the next one. I see why you would want to protect your daughter from me. I'm no saint. But, I'm not the monster they're trying to make me out to be. I never raped anybody in my life. I have to clear my name."

He shook his head. "I don't think clearing your name is what you should be worried about. The Davidsons are a very ruthless and powerful family. They have decided that you are no longer welcome here. It's time for you to leave Jamaica, Tarzan. You have to get out as soon as possible."

I knew that what he was saying made sense. Jamaica wasn't big enough for me and Dada. Not right now. I had made a total mess of everything since landing here. But, now I was at the point of no return.

"I'm not going anywhere, Bishop. I came here to Kingston to start over. I'm not going back to New York leaving all this stuff unresolved. I'm innocent. Your Bible has to say something about that, right? As an innocent man, I'm not running. I'm staying right here and I'm gonna clear my name. You don't have to worry about me. I might not be the righteous man you always talked about. But, there's always been some force out there watching over me. Guiding me. I'm gonna trust that same force to guide me now."

Bishop watched me for a moment, as if he was thinking about the whole thing. He nodded after a couple of minutes.

"God has a plan for everyone. Even when it doesn't seem like there's a plan, we are constantly being placed where we need to be at exactly the time we need to be there. There is no such thing as coincidence. Nothing is ever left to chance. And if you take heed you will see that your path is before you. God has already laid out a way of escape. Righteousness will always find its way."

I laughed. "Some path I'm on. Out on bail and on the run for rape. Doesn't really sound too righteous."

He nodded. "A real righteous man must live his life without reproach. He must face his problems with the faith that God will see him through. No matter what storms may come."

I laughed. "We keep talking about righteousness, Bishop. But, I'm starting to think that philosophy doesn't apply to me. Even when I try to do the right thing, I get punished for it. Kaydeen was the aggressive one, throwing herself all over me, and I made her stop because I'm in love with your daughter. That's the type of thing a righteous man might do. Now look where that got me."

Bishop thought about it for a while. He looked at me, intently.

"In the Bible, Joseph was falsely accused of raping Poti-phar's wife. Joseph had already been through more than his share of hardships in his life up to that point. His brothers had betrayed him. He had been thrown in a pit and left for dead. And eventually, he had been sold into slavery. Joseph was not living what you would consider a charmed life."

I was paying close attention to this story. This Joseph guy sounded like he had the same kind of luck I had.

"Joseph was accused of raping Potiphar's wife, even though he had never even touched the woman. She threw herself at him, the way you describe Kaydeen doing with you. But, Joseph resisted and was falsely accused. He was thrown in prison where everything seemed hopeless. But, God remembered Joseph and blessed him. Even down in the deep vestiges of that prison, God remembered him and gave him the power to understand dreams and visions. Turns out that the pharaoh was being tormented by some dreams that he kept having. Complicated dreams that he couldn't grasp the meaning of. Word got back to the pha-raoh that there was a man in his prison that could help him out. Joseph was able to interpret the pharaoh's dreams. Through those interpretations, Joseph became the king's trusted advisor and he eventually became the ruler of Egypt."

Bishop leaned in toward me. "My point is this, Tarzan. You have seen your share of trouble. Trouble that landed you in prison. Not just the kind with bars and gates." He gestured toward his temple. "The prison of your mind. But, you already have the tools you need to get out. God has already provided you with the skills necessary for you to open the gates of your prison. Use it to claim your throne."

I thought about it, piecing together the story Bishop had just told me and trying to understand how it related to me and my current situation. It certainly felt like I was stuck in the middle of a dream—a nightmare, really—that I couldn't tell the meaning of. I knew one thing for sure. If I was going to get out of the trouble I was in, I would have to do it on my own.

Outside the window, I could see people beginning to emerge from their homes to start the day. I knew that soon the church would be busy and the bishop would have visitors. I had to get moving before anyone discovered I was there.

"Bishop, I'm going to leave now." I looked at him, sadly. I wanted to ask him if he could go and summon Maya. Maybe she and I could steal a few sweet moments and I could tell her that I was sorry. But, I didn't want to put her in any danger. It felt like there was no place in the world that I belonged. I'd been drifting from one hiding place to the next. I was getting tired of running. But, the last thing I wanted to do was bring trouble to the bishop's and Maya's doorsteps.

"Thank you for everything." I realized that the man wasn't so bad after all. All he really wanted was to protect his daughter from any possible heartbreak. I had to respect that. Even if he had given me hell in the process. I wondered what it would have been like to grow up with a father figure like the bishop. Someone to give me structure, boundaries, and sound advice. Maya was blessed. I wondered if she realized that.

We both stood up. Face-to-face, we shook hands.

"Please let Maya know that I love her," I said. I had no idea when I would have a chance to see her again. It was way too dangerous now.

"I will," the bishop said. "Be careful, Tarzan."

WALK LIKE A MAN

I rode my bike way up into the mountains where Farmer lived. It was the only place I could think of where Dada and his goons might not look for me. Farmer had gotten most of his operation running after his release from prison. But, he had been keeping a far lower profile in the wake of the raids that dismantled my crew. I was the most sought-after man in Kingston at the moment, and I needed to get somewhere low and discreet with someone I could trust.

Farmer tucked me deep in the back of his ganja field, where I spent the whole afternoon in a lean-to shack, smoking spliff after spliff. Even in the haze of marijuana, my mind found no peace. I was in a fucked-up situation. My money was gone, I was on the run, and surely there was a price on my head. I was worried about my family. I missed my lady, and each time Maya crossed my mind, I got choked up. It was possible I might never see her again. The thought broke my heart.

What made it even harder to accept was the fact that all of this was my own fault. I had a woman in my life who carried herself like a queen. Maya was sweet, loyal, and supportive. Everything I ever wanted in a woman. She was the opposite of every loud, ghetto hood rat I ever dated before. And, despite the fact that I had been blessed with a woman like that, I had allowed myself to get distracted by a devilish imposter.

Kaydeen Davidson. When my thoughts drifted to her, and I imagined her face in my mind, I was filled with a fury that made me tremble. It was hard to imagine that I'd ever been attracted to her. I chastised myself for not seeing her cunning and manipulative ways sooner. She had fooled me into thinking that she was somehow different from her brother. In her eyes, even her cutthroat father was some kind of hero. Now, it was clear to me that she was a wolf in sheep's clothing. Her stunning physical beauty masked the ugliness of her true character. She was just like the men in her family. Probably even more vicious than they were. I laughed to myself now, realizing she had fooled me into believing that she was any different from the rest of the Davidson family. Like Dada and her father Pierce, Kaydeen was an evil puppet master who used people for her own enjoyment. Growing up, I'd been warned to never trust a big butt and smile. But, I had fallen for that anyway. Now it had cost me everything. I regretted ever giving that woman a moment of my time.

The situation couldn't have happened at a worse time. It was the night of the ten-million-dollar dancehall battle. As I looked down at the view of Kingston from Farmer's mountainside home, I knew I had to go back. There was no way I could let Killa Bean and the crew take that stage without me. Not when my boy had taken such a brutal assault because of me. Not when I had spent so much time perfecting the moves that I knew would win us that prize money. I had to face my problems with faith the way the bishop had described. I wasn't sure whether or not I would survive the night. There was a very real possibility I could be killed the moment I stepped back into Kingston. But, I had to go back. For my family and the people I loved. This was my chance to use my skills to escape my circumstances the way Joseph had in the Bible story the bishop told me.

I waited until I knew the dance clash was already in full swing. The Jungle would be packed with people from all over Kingston. This was a major event that had been all over radio and TV commercials for weeks. There would be television cameras, bright lights, and huge crowds. I prayed that those things would keep me from becoming a casualty on a public stage.

I knew my crew must be wondering where I was. They probably weren't expecting me to be there tonight. I hadn't spoken to them, let alone rehearsed with them, in days. I was the front man for our big routine. They couldn't perform the choreography we'd been practicing for this night without me in my spot at the front of our formation. I knew that the All Star Blazers would be one of the last crews to perform, so I bided my time. There was a lot riding on me tonight. I had to get to The Jungle by any means necessary.

I set out for Kingston hours after the party got under way. While I rode along the highway, I imagined the scene I would be walking into. Different Jamaican artists and stars were performing in between each dance crew. Beenie

Man, Sean Paul, Bounty Killer, Demarco, Bling Dawg, Voice Mail, T.O.K. I knew the crowd would be tremendous. I also knew that Dada would be in the building. Probably seated at his usual table in VIP with his goons around him. No doubt anticipating my arrival.

I sped along the highway, heading for the clash. The scenery whizzed past me and I felt my cell phone vibrating in my pocket. Toasta and Killa Bean had been calling me nonstop. I didn't answer, focused on getting to The Jungle. There was no time to talk now.

The closer I got to The Jungle, the more content I began to feel. I felt lighter than I had in days. My soul was at peace. I was alone on the road. Just me and my bike Dutty riding toward whatever destiny was mine. I began to think about my life so far. About how far I had come in the time since my release from jail. Part of me wondered whether coming to Jamaica had been a mistake. There was no question that my current circumstances were completely fucked up. But in spite of all the mayhem I had caused, there had been some wonderful moments since my arrival here. A mental slide show began to play of all the good times I'd enjoyed since I touched down in Kingston. Time spent loving Maya, laughing with Toasta, getting wisdom from Aunt Cheryl and Uncle Screechie. But it was the time I spent dancing with Killa Bean and the All Star Blazers that really stood out for me.

In the dance, I had discovered a part of myself that I never knew existed. Until Toasta and Maya introduced me to dancehall culture, I had no way to vent all the frustration, angst, rage, and power I felt inside of me. Dancing used to be a thing I frowned on. I thought it was fruity. But, now I knew that for me it was the highest form of self-expression. It was my therapy. On the dance floor was where I told my story. And tonight, I was anxious to get to The Jungle and let it all out.

An eerie silence surrounded me on all sides as I sped down the lonely highway toward the dancehall. I sensed that something was about to happen. Something big. It felt like there was a presence on the road with me. Some un-explainable force that was palpable. Without explanation, a feeling of complete peace washed over me. I could sense that tonight everything was going to happen exactly the way it was meant to.

I saw the blue lights flashing around me suddenly, and my heart raced. I was filled with instant dread. Then I heard the police sirens, and realized they were coming for me. I sped up, steering my bike like a madman. I was at peace with whatever happened tonight. They could lock me up, deport me, or do whatever they wanted. But, first I was determined to hit that dancehall stage with my crew.

With my adrenaline racing, I gripped the handle of my motorcycle tightly. There were three police cars chasing me now. I was grateful the highway was clear at this late hour. I hit each turn at maximum speed, praying the whole time that I didn't spin out. I was getting closer to The Jungle now and more police cars joined the chase. I saw the bright lights of the dancehall in the distance, and I gunned the engine, giving it all I had. The worst thing in the world would be to get this close and not make it. As I sped closer and closer to the dancehall, I could hear my mama's favorite phrase in my head.

The devil is a liar!

I could hear the crowd roaring inside the dancehall as I got closer. I prayed that by this time the All Star Blazers would be onstage. I sped through the parking lot with the police cars right behind me in hot pursuit. I headed for the front entrance on my motorcycle, revving the engine as a warning to anyone in my path. People jumped back out of the way as I raced into The Jungle, bringing my bike to a screeching halt right in the center of the dance floor.

I jumped off Dutty and got my footing. I looked around and sat that Killa Bean and the guys were in the middle of our second routine. I rushed toward them and joined The All Star Blazers, already in midroutine. The crowd was going off, as I caught step with the guys and nailed the moves. My entrance had been one for the record books. I knew there must be some who wondered whether it was all part of our routine. My eyes swept the crowd. I spotted the Dada Posse there, standing off to the side waiting for their turn. I had no idea that their crew and ours had been locked in a tough competition for quite a while now. The two crews had been battling hard for a minute, getting equal love from the crowd, and the vibe inside of the dancehall was intense. The crowd was still going wild in response to my dramatic entrance. I could see the relief on Killa's face, and the rest of crew. They were glad I was there—both for the sake of my own safety and for our chances of winning the battle. I caught sight of Dada standing near the railing up in VIP. He looked livid.

I danced my heart out. With all the energy I could muster, I pushed myself to the limit, each move executed with power and precision. All of my emotion poured forth.

Defiance, rage, triumph, strength, cockiness, and swag. We pulled out all of our best moves, while the crowd reacted with cheers and roars. Dada Posse didn't stand a chance.

Raddy Rich stepped forward and battled me one on one. He gave it all he had. I watched him, aware that his life depended on winning this clash. If Raddy Rich lost—especially to me, of all people—Dada would surely kill him. I watched him dance, while I backed up slowly until I was at the edge of the stage. Beenie Man stood onstage with his entourage preparing to perform. I locked eyes with him, resisting the urge to bug out a little bit that I was this close to a living legend. He watched me scamper up on the stage, and waved his goons back when they rushed toward me. He looked at me and gave me a head nod of approval. It was all the encouragement I needed.

I stood on the stage and waited for Raddy Rich to finish his routine. The second he hit his last step, I took a running leap off the stage and grabbed a hold of the lights wired above the crowd. I swung over the heads of the Dada Posse. Tarzan swinging across The Jungle. The volume and energy of the crowd was electric as I swung with all my might, landing right in front of Raddy Rich. I made a funny face, wiped imaginary dirt off my shoulders, and started doing Raddy's own dance right in front of him. The crowd erupted in chaos.

Raddy looked at me, stunned. He couldn't believe that I had taken his own move and flipped it on him. Killa Bean and the rest of the All Star Blazers joined in. Now we were all doing the Raddy Rich. In defeat, Raddy Rich took off his DADA POSSE jacket, tossed it aside, and joined us in the dance. We stepped in perfect synchronicity, with one soul. One rhythm. It was beautiful.

Complete anarchy erupted in The Jungle. Both crews did the dance together, killing the choreography. The crowd joined in, unified under one common banner for the first time all night. The energy in the room was out of this world, all of us on one accord.

The emcee took the stage.

"Kingston, I think we have a winner! The All Star Blazers! Ten-million-dollar dance clash winners!"

We all started cheering, jumping up and down, ecstatic. Toasta, Killa, and the crew all hugged each other and clapped hands. Beenie Man took to the stage, performing to a crowd that seemed ready to explode. Maya fought her way through the dense mob, and rushed to my side. She threw her arms around me so tightly that I nearly lost my balance. I could sense that she was happy I had won, but she was even more relieved to see me alive.

"Baby, you did it! You won!" Maya could barely believe it. Same here. She jumped into my arms, and I kissed her with all my might.

Toasta interrupted.

"Hate to be di one to end another Hallmark moment, brethren. But, we gotta roll." He gestured toward Casanova, standing near the entrance with his guards doing their best to keep the police at bay. I was grateful for Casanova putting it all on the line for my sake. I knew that he could only stall for so long. I had to get moving.

Maya clung to me, tightly. "Baby, wait." Her voice was filled with desperation. "I'm going with you."

I shook my head defiantly. "No. You're not!" I meant that shit. There was no way I was putting Maya in any more danger because of my own bad choices.

"We should go out the back way," Toasta said. "The front is all lit up with police lights." He started to lead the way toward the back of the club.

I stopped him. "No, bro. I got this. You stay." The last thing I was gonna do was put another one of my family members' lives on the line. This was my beef. My war. Not Toasta's. "Collect the prize money," I said. "Make sure you get that. I'm gonna sneak out the back alone. Don't worry. I'm good."

Toasta hesitated. He looked at me and narrowed his eyes, suspiciously. "You sure?"

I nodded. "Go get that ten million dollars. I'm gonna go underground. Lay low for a while. I'll get in touch with you in a couple of days when things die down."

"But, that's your money," Toasta said. "You're gonna need it. Can't make no moves empty-handed."

"That's *our* money," I corrected him. "We already discussed the plan. Nothing has changed. Give the guys their cut. And take my part and put that into your music. That's the wisest investment I can make right now. I believe in you. All Star Blazers, fam. We in this together."

He hugged me. I leaned in and whispered to him, "Make sure you take care of my mama."

He looked at me, a slight frown on his face. I could sense that he wanted to protest. But, time was running out and we both knew I had to get up out of there. Finally, he nodded.

"You'll take care of her yourself. When you get back."

I shook his hand hard. I hoped that was how this all played out.

"Respect, Tarzan. Bless up."

I turned to face Maya. She was fighting back tears. One fell, and I wiped it away.

"Don't do that," I said. "I'm coming back." I kissed her again. "I'm so sorry for everything, Maya. I'm a fool and I made a whole bunch of stupid mistakes. But, I didn't rape nobody. You gotta believe that."

She nodded. "I know you, Tarzan. You wouldn't do anything that savage."

I looked at her, so much regret in my heart. She did know me. Better than anybody. And I believed that I really knew her, too. No matter what secrets she might have kept from me. I knew her heart.

"I love you, Maya."

She forced a smile. "I love you, too."

I fought my way through the pressing crowd and ran toward the back exit. One of Casanova's guards cleared a path, leading me out a door that led to an alleyway on the far side of the lot. Once the night air filled my lungs, I took off. I was running at first, as fast as I could. I was desperate to put as much distance between me and the cops as possible. I wasn't sure how I would get out of town now that my bike was parked in the center of The Jungle, right in the middle of all the police activity. I slowed to a walk, as I thought about my next move.

I heard the faint sound of footsteps behind me, and an incredible wave of dread washed over me. The night seemed to grow even darker, and the hairs on the back of my neck stood at attention. I could sense the presence of a dark and

looming spirit surrounding me. This was the exact opposite of the feeling of calm I had experienced earlier on the
roadway. This energy was evil.

Sure enough, Dada's voice pierced the silent darkness.

"Turn around," he called out to me.

I kept walking. I thought about my mama's prayers. The
ones she often uttered as I went out into the mean streets
of Brooklyn.

Lord, please protect him from dangers seen and unseen.

I began to say that one silently as I walked.

"Mi say turn around, Yankee boy!"

I kept walking, unfazed. If this was it, I was ready. Fuck
it. I was tired of running. From the police and the gangs
back in Brooklyn, from the cops here in Kingston, and
from this bitch ass nigga Dada standing behind me demand-
ing me to obey him. Fuck that. My name was Tarzan. I was
a king. Not nobody's boy.

I felt the impact of the bullet before I heard the first shot.
I was jolted by the pain as it tore through my body. But, there
was no time to react before the next one hit me, followed by
several more. As each bullet made impact with my body, I
forced myself to keep walking. Blood began to ooze forth
from me, leaking all over the pavement. My ears were ring-
ing, and I felt a cold sweat washing over me from head to toe.

I kept walking, Bishop's words in my ears.

"The steps of a righteous man are ordered by the Lord."

With each step forward, I knew I had done my best. Far
from perfect. But, I had given it my best shot. I tried to do
something meaningful for my family. Tried to be a better
man and to make my mama proud. My conscience was
clear.

I grew weaker with each stride. My vision grew blurry, and the sounds around me became muffled. I felt myself falling slowly to the ground with my eyes wide open. I hit the pavement and watched my life slip away on the hard, cold streets of Kingston.

KING OF THE JUNGLE

I wish there were a way for spirits to speak to the people they leave behind. I wish I could tell Maya that I'm always there, watching her and still missing her so deeply that it hurts sometimes. I wish I could tell her that her father had been right all along. Not just about the values he raised his daughters to uphold. But about God and how real He is. How our prayers get answered in the strangest ways. I never knew that even when things were going horribly wrong in my life, I was being directed to a destiny that was greater than I had ever dreamed.

A month after my spirit left my body, my cousin recorded a song dedicated to me called "King of the Jungle." He poured his heart and soul into that song, making it his final grand gesture to the cousin he loved. The song went straight to number one in Jamaica, bolstered by the folklore of Tarzan—the Yankee boy from Brooklyn who rose from yard to become King of the Dancehall. The song became an instant classic.

Just as I had asked him to, Toasta looked after my mother. He sent her money, paid her doctor's bills, and finally got her out of the projects. Trent finished college, got a great job, and was doing well on his own. He did everything in his power to make our mama proud.

Toasta and his family moved out of their little zinc house and into a huge home on the far side of Kingston. Bishop blessed the place before they moved in, and the home was filled with the usual laughter, music, and dance. The kids grew up in a much happier, healthier environment than the struggle they had known in the years before their father's success. Aunt Cheryl fixed up her home in Hellshire and even found love again. A grocer at the market fancied the way her hips swayed when she walked the aisles.

The bishop looked after Maya and my son, Tarzan, Jr. That's what I mean. It's funny how God works. Ironically, Maya had gotten pregnant the very first time we made love. Unbeknownst to either of us, as I exited the world, she was in the early stages of bringing a new life into it.

I found out that God has a sense of humor, too. My son inherited all the traits the bishop despised in me. Tarzan, Jr. is stubborn, fearless, and has some pretty mean moves on the dance floor. Bishop often interacts with his grandson, his lips pulled into a reluctant grin as he admires the young man's grit and energy. It makes me marvel at how awesome the creator is. How everything works together for good.

Maya was my soul mate. I found that out after I messed everything up by getting tangled up with Kaydeen. It was true that Maya had deceived me. But, it never affected her love for me. My ego had been too bruised for me to see that. My anger had clouded my judgment, leaving me ripe for the devil's picking. That devil—Kaydeen—had enticed me with her strange and bitter fruit. I had nearly fully taken the bait. But, I paid the ultimate price anyway.

Still, I feel like I somehow passed the test. The old me would have made an even bigger mess than the one I made. It was my love for Maya that caused me to reject Kaydeen. Something in me had changed. Maya's love, and the dream of a future with her, made me try to be a better man. To be a king.

Some people think my story is a sad one. I guess in some ways, it is. But, I see it as a story of triumph. Over my demons, over the Davidson family and all their evil intentions. They may have buried me. But, they never understood that I was a seed. A seed of righteousness, flourishing through the blood of my son, the heart of my family, and the soul of dancehall.

Television and radio host, comedian, actor, producer, rapper, writer, director, DJ, philanthropist, children's book author, and activist NICK CANNON has entertained audiences for more than twenty years. Nick is best known for his work as creator, host, and executive producer of MTV's sketch comedy show *Wild 'N Out*, currently airing its eighteenth season. He is currently the executive producer and host of Fox's hit TV series *The Masked Singer* and is the host and producer of the nationally syndicated radio show *Nick Cannon Radio*. He is also the producer, writer, director, and star of the films *She Ball* and *Miracles Across 125th Street*. Simultaneously, the entertainment mogul has been a musician for more than thirty years. As a music business curator and label head of Ncredible Entertainment, Nick has helped discover and develop award-winning talent such as H.E.R. and Kehlani while continuously curating a roster of groundbreaking talent that will dominate the airwaves and music landscape. He is the father of eight and is a creative and entrepreneurial force at the vanguard of his generation, with more than seventeen million subscribers.